Praise for Bianca D'Arc's
Maiden Flight

"*Maiden Flight* is an erotic romance with plenty of adventure and fantasy. Bianca D'Arc is a master at weaving a story full of fantasy and adventure that leaps off the page."

~ *Fresh Fiction*

"Maiden Flight is the first book in the Dragon Knights series and is a fast-paced read that kept my interest throughout. [...] I am looking forward to learning more about these knights and some of their ladies in the future..."

~ *Literary Nymphs Reviews*

Look for these titles by
Bianca D'Arc

Now Available:

Maiden Flight

Bianca D'Arc

SAMHAIN
PUBLISHING

Samhain Publishing, Ltd.
11821 Mason Montgomery Road, 4B
Cincinnati, OH 45249
www.samhainpublishing.com

Editing by Amy Sherwood
Cover by Angela Waters

This book has been previously published and has been revised from its original release.
First Samhain Publishing, Ltd. electronic publication: August 2012
First Samhain Publishing, Ltd. print publication: September 2013

Dedication

This book is dedicated first and foremost to my mother, who helped me discover the dragon within myself. She was a fierce advocate of education and pursuing your dreams— whatever they may be. Thanks, Mom, for always believing in me and teaching me by example. I miss your loving friendship and wise counsel, but I know you're still guiding my path from realms beyond mortal comprehension.

I also want to thank my Dad for not giving up on me, or on himself, after losing the love of his life. It takes a strong man to love a strong woman and an even stronger man to survive losing her all too soon. They had fifty-four happy years together and their love is the touchstone from which our whole family learned what true love is really all about. Thanks, Dad, for sticking with me. Neither of us ever expected things to go this way, but I'm glad I've had a chance to get to know you better over the past few years.

Chapter One

Belora tracked the stag through the forest. Carefully chosen for this hunt, the stag was older, past the prime of his life, and would feed her small family of two for more than a month if she and her mother used it wisely. On silent feet, she followed him down to the water, a small trickle of stream that fed into the huge lake beyond.

Taking careful aim with her bow, Belora offered up a silent prayer of hope and thanks to the Mother of All and to the spirit of the stag that would give its life so that she and her mother could live. She loosed the arrow, watching it sail home to her target, embedding itself deep in the stag's heart. Her aim was true.

As expected, the stag ran off, pumping away the last of its life in a desperate attempt to escape. She followed, saddened by the poor creature's flight but knowing it must be so. The old stag ran into a clearing, flailing wildly. He was nearing his end, she knew, and again she prayed to the Mother of All that it would be swift.

The stag faltered in its running stride, a shadow seeming to pass over from above. A moment later, the stag was gone, clasped tightly in the talons of a magnificent dragon winging away toward the far end of the small clearing.

Belora took off as fast as her tired feet would carry her, following the dragon who had stolen her prize.

Coming out of his swooping dive, the dragon pinned the stag's quivering body between the long talons of his right foreleg. He'd made a clean kill, stabbing the beast through the heart with his sharp-edged digit even before lifting it into the air. It struggled for a few moments more, then lay dead in his grasp. The dragon rejoiced in the skillful kill, chortling smoke into the air above him.

He came to a neat landing at the far end of the small clearing and dropped the dead stag to the ground with satisfaction. That was when he noticed the little stick protruding from the other side of the beast. It was an arrow. Drat.

"Oh no, you don't!"

The irate, high-pitched human voice made the dragon shift his gaze upward to look quizzically at the small female now facing him with her hands perched in tight fists on her hips. A longbow was slung over her shoulder.

"I shot that stag well before you swooped down and picked him up. He's my kill. What's more, he will feed me and my mother for a month or more. For you, he's just a snack! You leave him be. He's mine."

She shook with indignant anger and it was truly a sight to behold. Luminous green eyes sparkled in her pretty, flushed face. She seemed to have no fear of him, mighty dragon that he was, with blood on his talons and fire in his belly. She clearly had courage, and it impressed him. Few humans, much less small females, dared to deal with dragons directly.

He could feel her anger, and a rudimentary channel of thought opened between her mind and his. She was one of the rare humans then, who could communicate with his kind. This intrigued him even more, and one thought kept running through his mind—Gareth had to see this.

"What's your name, pretty one?" The dragon spoke directly into Belora's mind, surprising her a bit, but her mother had

told stories about the dragon she'd known as a child. Belora knew dragons communicated with humans mind to mind. It was part of their ancient magic.

"I'm Belora." She renewed her forceful stance. She could not let this dragon sense any fear. She needed that stag. "Will you yield the stag to me?"

"Why are you not afraid of my kind? Do you know dragons?"

That wasn't an answer, but she supposed she should at least be polite. Her mother had taught her the etiquette required when dealing with dragons.

"Not I, sir. My mother knew a dragon once though. She told me about your kind." Belora knew she had to convince him soon. The longer this dragged on, the more likely he was to haul her before some tribunal for poaching. "So what about the stag?"

"From where I stand, it was my talon that made the kill. Not your puny arrow. But you have a good argument. I'll give you that."

The dragon moved closer to her as she fumed in response, but she didn't realize she was being set up until it was much too late. While she argued with him, the dragon moved closer still, until he had the stag wrapped in the talons on one huge foreleg and she was much too close to the other. As she realized her mistake, he swooped in and made his move.

He reached out quicker than thought and snapped the padded digits of his left foreleg around her waist, trapping her arms inside the cage his wickedly sharp talons made around her. She screamed in frustration and more than a bit of fear. The dragon only chuckled.

"Don't worry, little one." His voice was gentle in her mind, as if trying to calm her.

The dragon beat his huge wings two or three times and then they were airborne. She couldn't help the little yelp of

11

fright that escaped as her feet left the ground. He could easily open his claw and drop her to the ground far below. *That would solve his problem quite easily*, she thought with growing horror.

But dragons were supposed to be noble creatures! In all the tales she'd heard about them, she'd never heard of one going to such lengths to toy with a human before. They were mankind's friends, not enemies, and they weren't supposed to go around snatching up maidens only to hurtle them to their deaths.

As they gained altitude and he did not release her to die a nasty and painful death, she began to calm. She was held in one front claw, the slain deer in the other. She looked around and realized she had never seen such a beautiful sight. The view from above was breathtaking. She could see the huge mountain lake as they approached it, and if she craned her neck to look behind, she could see the forest canopy, green and fertile, hiding the secrets of the creatures that lived within.

She and her mother lived there, under the thick cover of trees, and had for many years. It was their haven, their home. Nothing as magical as this had ever happened to Belora, living isolated in the forest, and she decided to enjoy this moment out of time, flying high above the world. She would likely never have the chance again, for it was rare that a dragon transported a human that was not their knight partner. She knew that from the stories and legends the old ones told of knights and dragons. Even her mother—who had been friends with a dragon in her youth—had never flown with one. It was a rare and magical experience.

"Do you like the view, little one?"

"It's beautiful!" Belora had to shout to be heard over the racing wind.

The dragon chuckled, thoughtfully directing the stream of smoke out behind him and away from her. She realized from the gesture that he was well used to being around humans and carrying them as he flew, but she guessed he didn't carry too many in his claws. The legends all said knights rode on the backs of their dragon partners.

"Where are you taking me?" She pulled her attention from the gorgeous vista long enough to question her predicament. If he was taking her to a tribunal, she was in big trouble. She'd rather know now if she would be facing arrest when they landed.

"Fear not, little one. I said you had a good case for the stag. We will let the knight decide."

They cruised over the edge of the large mountain lake. The water sparkled below as the dragon dropped lower. A moist breeze off the water teased her senses.

"What knight?" That didn't sound good.

Rather than calming her fears, the news that there was a knight in the area only made things worse. She'd been poaching, plain and simple. Mere peasants weren't allowed to kill the deer to feed their families, but the dragons were welcome to them as a snack at any time.

"That knight," the dragon thought back at her. It took her a moment to understand his meaning, but when she looked down and just ahead of their path, she saw a sleek male body cutting through the waters of the lake. He swam like a fish or like one of the great sea creatures she had heard stories about. She found herself distracted by the sun gleaming off the powerful muscles of his arms as he sliced through the water, heading for shore. Something about the man's hard body pulled at her most feminine core, though she was inexperienced with men, in general.

"I am Kelvan and that's Gareth, my knight."

Her eyes followed the man cutting through the waters below. She'd never seen a dragon in person before, much less a knight. Surprisingly, the hard-muscled man intrigued her even more than the amazing blue-green dragon who spoke so

13

effortlessly in her mind.

The thought gave her pause. She'd met any number of men from the nearby village and never had such a reaction to the mere sight of one, but this man was different. Without even seeing his face clearly, she felt something deep down inside her stir to life. It was as if something in him called out to her—to the deep parts of her femininity that had never been awakened before. She wanted to know this man. She wanted to see him smile, and she wanted to know what those wetly gleaming muscles would feel like under her hands.

The thought shocked her. Shocked, and excited, if she were being honest. The thought of his strong arms wrapped around her made her insides quiver. The thought of his lips trailing over her untried body caused moisture to blossom between her thighs. She felt desire for this unknown man, the likes of which she had never experienced, but oh, how she wanted to experience it now!

The scandalous thought roused her from her contemplation of the handsome man. He was just a knight, she tried to tell herself. She didn't even know him. He would probably be old and unattractive when she finally saw his face clearly. No matter what she tried to tell herself, though, she kept looking back at the man cutting through the water so effortlessly, as if drawn. She tried to shake off the almost magnetic pull he had on her, but it was surprisingly hard to gather her wits.

"You're a fighting dragon, then?"

The dragon didn't grace her obvious statement with an answer.

"There are no dragon enclaves this far east. Where do you hail from?"

"Not that it is any of your business, but the king has asked us to set up a new Lair just to the south of here. You will be seeing more of us patrolling the skies in the days to come."

"But why?" His startling news was enough to make her forget the knight for the moment. "The border with Skithdron has been peaceful for many years."

She knew it had not always been so. Wild skiths—snake-like creatures that were as large as dragons and spit deadly burning venom—were often found along the border, harrying herds and killing unsuspecting farmers who crossed their path.

The native skiths gave the neighboring kingdom its name and heraldic symbol, much as the dragons were the symbol of her land, but that's where all similarity ended. Dragons were reasoning creatures of high intelligence, where skiths were pack hunters intent only on killing and destruction.

It was rumored they could be herded against an enemy, and in legends of older times, it was believed this border region had been deliberately decimated by herds of skiths. They'd been sent as a first wave by the neighboring army that had almost taken the region completely. The only thing that saved the land had been the native dragons, fighting the hated skiths back with flame. Dragons were the only thing a full-grown skith was afraid of.

The blue-green dragon who held her prisoner directed a stream of rumbling smoke away from her as he scoffed at her words. Her mother had warned her that when dragons became angry they sometimes had a hard time controlling their fire.

"Skithdron has a new king. One not worthy of the title. War is coming. It is only a question of when." Again there was a belch of smoke that he thoughtfully directed out behind them as he flew.

"I didn't know." She tried to quell the frightened quaver in her voice as she shouted to be heard over the rushing wind.

She knew things had to be serious indeed if the king had sent a contingent of knights and fighting dragons to make their home on the border. Her chest tightened as she realized they all could be in serious danger. She and her mother might have to flee yet again, losing the snug little home in the forest that had sheltered them safely for so long.

"Thank heaven the king sent you here. We're all but unprotected here on the border."

"Not anymore." The dragon seemed to chuckle and preen as he circled lower, searching for the perfect landing site.

"Gareth, I've got a live one here." The dragon communicated telepathically with his partner, who still swam through the waters below.

"You found your deer, then? I'm almost through with my swim. We can get back underway as soon as you finish your snack."

"Not quite." The dragon swooped lower as he prepared to land on the far shore. *"There was a poacher there before me and we quarreled over the kill. I've brought her to you to decide who keeps the stag."*

"Her?"

"Indeed," the dragon replied dryly. *"She has no fear of my kind and the ability to communicate with us, too. I thought you ought to see her before we departed."*

"Intriguing." The knight neared shore as the dragon landed lightly, setting both the deer and his wriggling human burden down on the ground, gentle as could be.

"Hmm. Beautiful too. And feisty."

"Beautiful?"

"In the way of humans. Quite beautiful, I believe. And quite upset with me. She did not come willingly."

The dragon released her, sat back, and watched the little human fume at him. She raged and paced, shrieking about being taken away by force, against her will, but the dragon paid her words no mind. Gareth would sort her out soon enough. In the meantime, it was quite amusing to watch with her antics.

Gareth got his first look at the woman—girl, really—as he walked out of the lake. The cool wetness of the water as it sluiced down his limbs barely registered in his mind as he strode toward the girl. She stomped around, ineffectively arguing in front of the impassive dragon.

Gareth was struck by her lithe form, her soft hair waving in the warm summer wind and the passion in her stance. She showed absolutely no fear of Kelvan, his dragon partner, though the beast outsized her many times over. No, this little woman was fearless and rather focused in her anger.

She was also too thin. It was more than obvious that she needed that stag to feed herself and her family. If they were all as thin as she was, they needed much more than just the one stag. Perhaps he and Kelvan could do something to help her the next time they came this way, he thought absently, not even realizing he was already looking forward to the next time he would see the girl.

He knew almost immediately that he wanted to see her again. Something about her drew him. There was a light in her, a fire that called to him. He didn't understand it, but it was beyond question. She pulled him in like a moth to a flame and he went willingly. The fire in her glittering green gaze mesmerized and the vulnerability in her bowed lips made him want to fall to his knees and give her everything he had, everything he was. The desire to please her, to protect her and cherish her, blindsided him. He didn't even know her. Yet everything about her called to him. He watched as she berated the dragon—or tried to. Kelvan seemed just as in awe of her as he was.

She had worked up a good head of steam as he neared, though she seemed completely unaware of his approach. Kelvan shifted his head, finally alerting her to Gareth's presence. She turned to face him, gasped, and suddenly stopped talking.

Maybe it was because he was naked, he realized belatedly, enjoying the way her eyes seemed glued to his groin. Of course, such attention caused his staff to grow rapidly, as did the enchanting stain of embarrassment on her cheeks. Slowly, he reached for his clothing. It lay in a pile only feet from where she stood, still watching him.

"Keep looking at me like that, mistress, and you will reap the consequences."

The girl gasped as her gaze shot up to his. Finally. Her mouth closed with a snap as she seemed to gather her wits.

"Your pardon, my lord, but I'm not used to meeting unclothed knights of the realm."

Sarcasm fairly dripped from her words. She wasn't afraid of him. Quite the contrary. He grew even more intrigued. Gareth shrugged into his shirt, leaving it unlaced for the moment as he faced her, now clothed more decently in breeches and shirt.

"My partner here tells me you claim this very large stag as your kill."

He thought his statement masterfully done, complimenting her hunting skill while making no mention of the fact that they all knew she had been poaching. That she was in the wrong, according to the law, bothered him much less than the thinness of her lithe little body. He would rather she take the deer and feed herself and her family. Kelvan could always hunt another or wait until they arrived back at the Lair to feed fully. He knew from long association with dragonkind that it would be no hardship for the huge creature who was his dearest friend in the world and closest companion.

"I shot him fair and square before this great lug lumbered in from above."

"Lumbered! I'm insulted. I never lumber."

"Mistress—" Gareth shook his head theatrically. "You have insulted a dragon. That is never wise."

The petite beauty looked up over her shoulder at the dragon and rolled her eyes.

"All right then, how about if I said you swooped in majestically?" She paused to see the dragon's reaction and then went for the kill. "And stole my deer."

Kelvan snorted, careful to keep his flame away from the humans, though he choked the woman momentarily with his sooty wheeze. While she coughed, Gareth smiled up at his partner.

"This is a strange one indeed. And just as beautiful as you said."

"She lights your fire, then?"

Gareth had to fake a cough to hide his start of laughter. *"Indeed."*

"Good. You need a hard fuck. You've been much too tense lately. I'll go hunt another deer while you settle things with Belora."

"*Belora*," Gareth repeated. It fit her, rolling through his mind as prettily as she stood before him. It was a delicate name. An intriguing name.

Kelvan winged away without responding, blowing the slight woman straight into his knight's arms, belching dragon laughter as he headed back toward the forest. The girl looked up at the knight, clinging to him to hold her steady in the fierce wind created by the dragon's massive wings.

"Where's he going?"

Gareth smiled down at her, holding her tightly in his arms. "To hunt another deer. You can have the stag, with our compliments."

Her whole face lit up with joy, and it was a sight to behold.

19

This young woman possessed more than mere beauty. She had a light that radiated from within, the likes of which he had seldom seen before. A rare jewel, indeed, and he knew he must have her, if only for this moment.

"Really?" Her wide eyes held hope for the first time since he'd encountered her, and happiness that made her glow.

"Yes, really." He tightened his arms around her, his gaze falling to her lips. He felt her breathing hitch as her body responded to his nearness. It was a good sign, as was the fact that she wasn't trying to get free from his embrace. Rather, she seemed comfortable in his arms, clinging to him in a way that was most gratifying. "Kelvan and I will fly you back to your home and deliver the deer there for you. Later."

"Later?" Her voice was soft as her eyes spoke of the pleasure he was bringing her with the soft, circular motions of his hands on her back.

"Much later."

His head dipped and his lips claimed hers in a sweet kiss that swiftly turned passionate. Gareth had only meant to give her a quick buss, then sit her down and discuss her family situation. As a knight of the realm, he couldn't let people go hungry. He'd wanted to help her, if he could.

But her kiss brought something to life inside him that would not be denied. She was sweet, but it was more than that. Her taste and innocent, passionate response brought out a possessiveness in him that he hadn't expected.

He wanted her. Despite the dragon's parting words, he hadn't meant to actually take her. But the feeling inside him was demanding more. Truth be told, it was demanding all. All he was. All he would ever be. All they could be together.

There was an instant recognition. An instant wanting. Needing. It was something Gareth had heard about, but never thought he would actually experience. This woman tasted like his true mate. The one woman meant to share his life. Knights often knew on the first meeting the woman meant for them. It was a blessing and a curse all knights shared. The magic of their dragon partners helped them recognize the woman that would make their extended family whole.

Gareth very much feared—and hoped—that Belora was that woman. His woman.

He pushed her further than he'd intended, needing to find out for certain. He'd make sweet love to her, fulfilling the driving need in his soul and then he'd know for sure. And then...well, he'd have to deal with the next part as it happened.

Convincing a woman to give up all she'd ever known to come live in a dragon's Lair probably wasn't the easiest thing in the world, but he'd faced bigger battles in his time. If Belora was the one, he'd move heaven and earth to keep her with him.

Gareth deepened the kiss. Though willing, the hesitancy with which she followed his passion told him a great deal. She was quite obviously untried, but willing. He pulled back after a long satisfying time but didn't release her. He needed to convince her, gently. Gareth would have to use all his rusty charm to entice her into his bed.

"You are very beautiful, Mistress Belora." He caressed her hair with one rough hand. She blushed so prettily he had to bend down and kiss her again. Her shy response enchanted him and reminded him how inexperienced she truly was. A man of the world could always tell. He pulled back and smiled to soften his words. "You're very young, sweetheart."

"Not too young, surely." There was a teasing challenge in her tone. "I have eighteen winters."

Gareth clicked his tongue and shook his head. "Just a babe, you are."

"How old are you, then? You can't be that much older than me. I won't believe it. You're in your prime." Her gaze walked over him, heating his blood. She was definitely attracted to him. That would make his goal easier.

"I take that as a compliment, mistress, that you think me prime. I feel like an old man compared to you."

"Not too old." She chuckled as he squeezed her playfully. He liked her sense of humor and the sparkle in her gorgeous green eyes.

"Never too old to appreciate a beauty such as yours. A man would have to be dead not to want you." He gave her a little harsh truth as he pressed his suit.

She gasped as his hands stroked intimately down her back and cupped the curve of her ass. He pulled her against his hard frame, letting her know how much he wanted her. The next move he would leave up to her. She was so young and obviously untried. He would have to give her some choice, but he prayed to the Mother of All that she would choose to make love with him. He needed her on a soul-deep level. He needed to know if she was the one. He thought he'd go mad if she turned him away now.

"And do *you* want me, sir knight?" The coquettish smile in her eyes was promising.

He actually growled as he ground his hips against hers. "I want you more than any woman I've ever known."

"Pretty words, sir," she replied slowly, her gaze measuring his response suspiciously. "I bet you've said the same to many a maid." She laughed as he stroked his hands upward to frame her face.

"I've never said anything of the kind. For that matter, I've never felt this way before. You have my word as a knight of the realm. You are special, Belora. I know we've only just met, but I feel as if I've known you all my life. As if I've been waiting for you." He felt his heart lodge somewhere in his throat as he gazed down into her mesmerizing green eyes. "Tell me you feel the same."

Her expression sobered and her breath caught. A dazzling light came from her beautiful eyes that humbled him.

"I thought I was being fanciful." Her whispered words made something fragile inside him tremble. "You truly feel it too?"

He kissed her lips sweetly. "I do."

"What does it mean?"

"It could mean everything, sweet Belora. Everything."

Nearly overcome by the thought, he lowered his mouth to hers again. His kiss was filled with savage intent as she clutched at his arms. His hands roamed over her lithe body, stroking her curves and supporting her when she sagged against him. At length, he broke away from the drugging ecstasy of her kiss.

"Will you lie with me, beautiful Belora?" His words were impassioned whispers against the soft, warm column of her neck. "Will you give me the gift of your body?"

She pulled back and it nearly killed him to let her draw even slightly away.

"I've never been with a man, Gareth." His heart stopped beating as he waited for her hesitant words. "But my mother's a healer. I know what to expect." She looked adorably hesitant at first, but she seemed to grow more certain with every word she spoke. A bit of the steadfast huntress Kelvan had encountered came to the fore, attracting him even more. "I want to be with you, Gareth. Will you teach me what I need to know to please you?"

He hugged her close. Uncustomary tears formed behind his eyes as he realized the import of this moment. This small woman's trust meant more to him than anything in the world— except perhaps for his bond with Kelvan.

But this encounter with Belora was nearly on the same

level. That alone told him this was a special moment. And a special woman. He'd be damned if he hadn't just found his mate.

It was a heady thought. A frightening thought. A thought for later consideration. Much later. For now, he had to concentrate on the beautiful woman in his arms.

"You need do nothing but be yourself to please me, sweet Belora."

Words failed him at that point, so he turned his attentions to showing her how beautiful she was. He lifted her rough tunic slowly over her head, enjoying her maidenly blushes. He'd never had a maiden before, but he had bedded many experienced women and knew how to please them. He would make certain this first time for Belora was as good as he could possibly make it. He wanted her to remember this encounter with joy.

When she was bare, he laid her down on the soft pile of their discarded clothing. She was noticeably shy, but willing. Her expression told him how much she wanted this, even if she'd never done it before.

He stroked her breast with one large hand. He was a big man, but he could be gentle when he needed to be and this was one of those times. At least for now, he would give her gentleness. If it turned out she could handle more, he would give it to her later, by all means. With pleasure.

She shivered as he stroked down to the point of her breast, pinching her pert nipple with just enough force to make her squeal with pleasure. He leaned lower and replaced his hands with his lips. Sucking her deep into his warmth, he watched as her gaze followed his movements. She looked both shocked and eager for more. The lovely flush in her cheeks indicated her rising desire.

"Gareth!" she keened as he sucked gently on her nipple, releasing her with a pop to pay the same homage to her other breast.

His hands were busy learning the curves of her waist, her hips, her thighs and what lay between. One hand parted the neat curls above her mound and found its way into her slick folds while she squirmed. He lifted his head and watched her carefully as he drew her nipple between his teeth with a little edge of roughness. From the way her fingers ran through his hair and drew him closer, she definitely liked what he was doing to her. No, she *loved* what he was doing to her. She shivered with delight each time he touched her.

"You'll never regret giving yourself to me, Belora. I swear it on my honor."

"The only way I'll regret this is if you stop now, Gareth." Her voice was deliciously breathy.

He almost laughed at her honest, soul-baring answer. This was a woman who wasn't afraid to take life by the horns. He was half in love with her already and they'd only really just met.

"I'd never leave you wanting, sweet Belora. I need you every bit as much as you probably need me by now."

"No one could need you more than I. It's not possible. What have you done to me, Gareth? What kind of magic is this?"

She gasped as he moved the hand he'd kept between her legs, teasing her clit. Holding her gaze, he slid one large, thoroughly wet finger into her core and watched carefully as he stretched tissues that had never known the touch of a man. The thought excited him beyond reason, but he held tightly to his control. This woman was special. He would make sure she enjoyed every moment they had together.

"It's the purest form of magic, sweet. The magic of man and woman."

He leaned in close and kissed her deeply, catching her cries of excitement in his mouth as he added a second finger inside her tight channel. He knew it might hurt her, but she was so deep in her pleasure, she was beyond pain now. This first time it would be a blessing to her to break through her barrier fast before she had time to worry and tense up. She was in the perfect place now, if he could just keep her there until he was buried deep inside her.

He slid over her, placing himself between her spread thighs, holding her gaze and doing his best to overwhelm her senses with deep, passionate kisses that kept her off balance. His fingers began pumping in and out of her channel, preparing her.

He brought his wet fingers to his cock and coated himself with her essence, hoping to make his passage easier on her this first time. Before she had time to think, he pressed forward, the cap of his raging erection sinking in with little trouble. He straightened over her, bracing his arms on either side of her face as he moved steadily forward.

"Do it now, Gareth. Come into me now!"

"Your wish," he surged forward, breaking through the barrier, "is my command." She jerked beneath him momentarily and he held still, watching the tightness around her sweet mouth ease as she got used to his presence in her body. "Better now?"

She tilted her head as if considering exactly how she felt. He loved that thoughtfulness about her. He loved her adventurous spirit. And he feared given half a chance, he would love her. Period.

"It feels odd, but very nice. Is there more?"

Gareth grinned down at her. "Much more. We've only just begun."

"Oh, good."

With a chuckle, Gareth began to move in her, watching her eyes light up as she discovered what came next. She was delightful to him. Fresh, eager and open to new experiences.

26

She was a treasure. He'd never felt so lighthearted while making love, never knew it could feel this right, this pure, this perfect.

She clamped her legs around him and he could feel her excitement rising fast. She was so responsive to him, it made it all that much better. He moved his hand between them and teased her clit until she tensed and cried out, experiencing her first orgasm while he remained hard within her. He watched her through it all, entranced by the look in her luminous eyes, the sheer pleasure on her pretty face.

He rode her throughout, helping her milk it for all it was worth. When she came back to earth, he was there, looking down into her beautiful eyes.

"Ready for more?" His smile teased her and she blushed so prettily he had to lean down and kiss her luscious lips. Rolling, he reversed their positions, keeping himself tight within her, watching the surprise enter her expression. "Do you ride?"

"We can no longer afford to keep a horse."

"Who needs a horse when you can ride me?" His teasing tone brought a spark of excitement to her eyes and she straightened, letting her beautiful breasts swing as she positioned herself atop him.

"Am I doing it right?" She began a slow up and down motion on him that made him groan in appreciation.

"Any righter and I'd be a dead man." His head flopped back to the ground as she increased her pace. "You're a natural, sweet. Keep on as you're going and we'll soon touch the stars together."

"Oh, Gareth!"

She was close. He could see it in the tensing of her sweet mouth. He moved his fingers up to cup her bouncing breasts, enjoying the look and feel of them in his hands as she rode him. He pinched her nipples and teased them with his thumbs, flicking them as she moved faster and faster in search of her goal.

"Come for me now, sweet. Let go and come now!"

She convulsed over him, straining as he pumped hard upward. He came with her, spilling a torrent of his seed within her tight depths.

"Oh!" She convulsed again as he watched, close to awe at the pleasure this small, untried woman had given him. He had never come so hard in his life. He emptied into her as if she had been made for him.

He stroked her hair, her back, her soft skin, even as his cock relaxed within her. Not seeing any reason to move further, he dragged a dry towel over her back and settled in for a short rest. He would have her again before this day was through, but for now she was wiped out.

Chapter Two

Belora woke on her back beneath Gareth, his cock hard once more within her. He stroked lightly, in and out, and she realized she was very wet and very excited. This man had shown her the most amazing things, and it seemed there was still more to learn. The heart-stopping attraction she had felt on first seeing him in the water now resolved into an awe-inspiring affection for the handsome, thoughtful man. He was so gentle with her, so caring in his way, yet so exciting. He'd shown her things about herself she had only been able to guess at before, and given her a new confidence in her femininity she had never had.

"About time you woke up." His soft grin eased the hard words.

She stretched, reaching out to stroke his stubbly cheek with one hand. She loved the masculine feel of him.

"Someone tired me out."

"Hmm. We'll have to see what we can do about that."

He rocked gently, in no hurry now to sate the hunger growing inside her. She climaxed twice before he let loose with his own completion, nearly drowning her in his seed. She knew a baby could come of what they'd just done but didn't care. Or rather, she kind of liked the idea of having this knight's baby, even if she never saw him again.

Here was a man worthy of fathering children. He was brave, strong, gallant and a considerate lover. She knew her initiation into sex could have been much more painful than it had been. In fact, aside from that one moment when he tore through her barrier, it had been nothing but pleasure.

No, if she got pregnant from this day's work, it was the will of the Mother. Such pleasure could not be wrong and if she had this man's child, the baby would be healthy, smart and as strong as its father. It would be a blessing.

"Come on, Belora." He tugged her to her feet, though the lethargy of good, hot loving weighed her down. She wanted to sleep again, but it seemed he wouldn't let her.

"Where are we going?"

"For a quick dip in the lake."

"What?" Her fatigue left in a rush. "That water's cold!"

"Invigorating," he countered, drawing her closer to where the clear waves lapped against the pebbly shore. "We need to clean you off or you'll be uncomfortable."

Her heart melted at his soft words. She realized then that he was caring for her again. He was the expert at sex and knew what was best for her. So far he had proven that he always put her pleasure and comfort before his own and that was a good quality in a man, she decided.

"Okay, but let's make this quick. I don't relish freezing my butt off."

He let her precede him so he could noticeably leer at the butt in question.

"No, that would be a definite shame. I'll make sure that your beautiful butt doesn't go anywhere, okay?"

He grabbed her ass in his warm hands and pushed her toward the clear water of the lake. They splashed in, laughing and smiling as he pulled her close. He took them only waist deep into the water before tugging her to a halt. Holding her eyes with his, he swept one hand down over her body and into the water, cupping between her legs. His calloused fingers teased through her folds. As he cleaned her, each sweep growing bolder, a fire kindled and leapt in her womb.

He plunged two fingers up into her sore channel, but backed off when she winced just the tiniest bit.

"I'm sorry," she said softly as he drew back.

"No, I should have realized you'd be sore after all we've done today."

"But I want more."

He shook his head with a soft smile. "You can't have it. Not that way at least."

"What other way is there?"

Now the fire returned to in his eyes. "There are many other ways, my sweet innocent."

"Not so innocent anymore, thanks to you, sir knight." She knew she was blushing from the heat rushing up her neck, but couldn't help it. Besides, he seemed to enjoy it as he touched the flush on her cheeks with one strong hand. His other hand lingered below the water, tracing her folds and soothing her aches with gentle touches.

"I doubt there's anything in this world that could take your innocence completely from you. It's part of your soul, shining out through your lovely eyes." He bent down and kissed her eyelids so softly it brought a tear to her eye.

She started to shiver but it wasn't from the cold.

"Let's get you out of the water. You're right. It is kind of chilly."

Instead of letting her walk out, he hoisted her up into his strong arms and carried her to shore. After drying her with his towel, he laid her down on the soft pile of their clothing and settled himself on his haunches between her bare legs.

"What are you doing?" She was just a bit nervous, lying there, so exposed to his gaze. Her eyes followed his every move, her mouth going dry and her stomach clenching in anticipation that was mixed with just a hint of fear. This was all so new to her, but this man, this moment, felt so right. The smile in his eyes reassured her, the passion in his gaze heated her blood.

"Just enjoying the view. You're gorgeous, Belora." He leaned forward and placed a smacking kiss on the soft swell of her tummy as she laughed. "And while I'm here, I might as well show you one of those other ways of giving pleasure. What do you say?"

He raised his gaze to meet hers and smiled in that devilish way of his that made her insides clench.

"I'm all for it. I think."

"Oh, don't worry. You're going to love this."

He moved downward, shocking her as his hands spread her pussy wide open and his tongue delved inside. She nearly bucked off the ground, the pleasure was so intense. He laved her most intimate places with his hot tongue, stroking down her slit and back up, pausing to seek inside the sore areas that had never known such passion before that day.

All pain was forgotten as shivers of delight danced up and down her spine. She'd never felt so wanton, so desirable as she did with this knight. He soothed her with long licks, exciting her with the odd foray to circle and tease her clit. Her legs trembled and her muscles went weak, anticipation building as he stroked her higher and higher.

"Gareth?" She didn't know how she could stand the sensations running through her body. It was frightening and profound at the same time.

"Shh, sweet. Just enjoy. This is for you." His whispered words brushed in soft puffs of heated air against her, making her even more eager. It wouldn't be long now.

She looked down and saw Gareth's sparkling eyes gazing up at her from between her legs. Something about the sight of him, pleasuring her so thoroughly and seeming to enjoy it, sent her soaring higher. When he bit down gently, but unexpectedly on her clit, she screamed and convulsed in yet another orgasm. He rode her through it, keeping his warm mouth on her.

"Gareth! Oh, Gareth." Whispered pleas escaped unnoticed from her lips as he curled her into his arms, much, much later. She could feel his hard cock against her, but he made no move to relieve his own tension.

When reason returned, she sat up and pushed him backward onto the bed of clothing. The surprise in his eyes made her bold.

"Surely if you can give me such pleasure with your mouth, I can do the same?"

Gareth placed his hands on her arms. "You don't have to do this, Belora. This last time was for you. I don't expect anything."

"Nonsense. I want to learn you the way you've learned me." She moved closer, settling closer to his thick erection. "I would take you in my body again, but I'm too sore. Let me do this for you, Gareth."

He let go of her arms and lay back with a silly grin on his face. "If you insist."

"Tell me what to do."

"Just touch me, Belora. Wrap your fingers around the base and suck the tip into your mouth. Use your tongue." She followed his instructions and was gratified to hear his harsh groan and feel the fingers tightening in her hair. He obviously liked what she was doing so she sucked harder. "Yes, just like that. Oh, Belora!"

She began to move her mouth on him in time with the tugging motions of his hand in her hair. He wasn't controlling her, but coaching her, she realized, and she took full advantage of his lesson to bring him to the brink of ecstasy.

At the same time, she was learning intimate things about

him. His musky scent, his salty taste, the rhythmic way he liked to be licked. She felt wicked and divine at the same time, learning how to pleasure a man such as this. She sucked lightly, then harder, following his cues as she learned the new landscape before her. Never had she imagined, even in her wildest dreams, taking a man in her mouth this way. It was something out of her realm of experience, but something she knew she wanted to do again. With this man, and this man alone.

"Let go now if you don't want me to come in your mouth," he warned. "I'm close."

But she wanted his come. She wanted it all. She wanted to taste him, to swallow him down, and take his essence into herself. She wanted all she could get of this noble, magnificent knight. For all too soon, she knew they would part and she might never see him again.

She sucked harder, and he gasped. That was all he could take. He tried to back away as he came, but she wouldn't let him. She hadn't expected to enjoy making him come as much as she had. Pleasing him had given her a sense of her own feminine power and allowed her to express the softer feelings she inexplicably had for this hard knight who had stolen her heart with only his smile.

They lay down together again for a while, basking in the lethargy that she was learning came after incredible sex. She enjoyed watching the late afternoon sun glinting off the lake and the dragon flying low over the forest in the distance. She felt secure and protected, held securely in her knight's embrace.

Belora turned in his arms to look up at his chiseled face. "You know, I've never seen a dragon in these parts before, much less a knight."

"You'll see more of us soon. We've founded a Lair just to the north of here by the king's command, and will be patrolling the border from now on."

"That sounds like trouble. Your dragon friend said we might see war from Skithdron." She really didn't like the implications of their presence on the border, though she was glad to have met this gentle, strong knight.

He nodded once. "It's true. There's unrest to the east. More skith attacks than usual for one thing, and political maneuvering between the kings and politicians."

"My mother said she'd heard rumors in the village, but we were hoping it was just talk."

"Unfortunately not."

She lay back against him, staring at the sky and thinking hard while he idly drew soft circles on her bare skin with his fingertips.

As the sun dipped lower in the sky, Gareth knew it was time to take her home. He didn't want to, but he had to do the right thing. She had family waiting. A mother who would worry if she didn't return that day.

What he wanted to do was kidnap her. Tie her to Kelvan's back and steal her away to the new Lair. But keeping her against her will wasn't the smartest way to begin what he hoped might be a long-term relationship. He had to let her go. For now.

Gareth shifted his weight and stood, sorting out their clothes. Belora stood as well, obviously taking her cue from him. They dressed silently, the oncoming chill in the evening air speeding their movements.

"Will I ever see you again?" Belora's tone was curious, not possessive, but the words caused a tightening in his heart.

"I hope I'll see you often." He took a chance, knowing he was rushing things. "In fact, I'd like you to come back with me to the new Lair, Belora. I want more than just this. Will you come with me?"

She took a moment before answering. Gareth didn't breathe, waiting for her response.

"I want to, more than you can know, but there's more to consider than just my desires." She looked down at her hands, wringing them with what looked like true regret.

"What could be more important than this?" He took her into his arms and skimmed her back with his fingers, bringing her close to his heart.

"My mother relies on me, Gareth." Her voice was small against his chest. "I can't just leave her."

Gareth set her back slightly so he could look into her eyes. "You are a noble creature, my Belora. Kelvan and I will take you home and speak with your mother. As Kel is fond of saying, the Mother of All will find a way." He stroked her cheek. "You're truly not afraid of him, are you?"

She gave him a puzzled smile. "Why would I be afraid of a dragon? They're noble creatures, especially those who serve the king and fight to protect us."

"And you can really hear him when he speaks to you?" Gareth held his breath. So much depended on her answer.

"Well, yes, of course. Can't everyone?"

He shook his head and laughed lightly. "Not everyone, Belora. Only a few are blessed with the ability."

She tilted her head, thinking. "That's strange. I thought everyone could. My mother can, I know that for certain. She was friends with a dragon when she was little."

He kissed her lightly. He looked forward to meeting Belora's mother. Women who could bespeak dragons were rare, in deed.

"Then the Mother of All has definitely put you in our path for a reason. If we are meant to be together—and I feel certain we are—then it will all work out. All I ask is that you at least agree to visit the Lair. I want you to see it and learn a little of our ways." He stroked her hair back from her face, his heart shining in his eyes. "If you think you could live there, well, then I'll have another question to ask you, but we'll take first things first. We'll check on your mother and then go for a visit, okay?"

"Okay. A short visit."

Adora watched in awe as a mighty dragon landed in the small clearing in front of her cabin in the woods. She'd not seen a dragon since she was a little girl, and this one was a beauty. Blue and green with the iridescent sparkle of his kind, this dragon reminded her of her childhood friend. Even more amazing, this dragon bore a young knight on his back along with her daughter! She wiped her hands on her apron and rushed out to greet them.

"Bel, my dear, you've brought guests." Adora smiled as her girl raced from the dragon's side to hug her.

"This is Gareth and Kelvan." Belora's excitement was evident as she took her mother's hands in hers, pulling her forward to meet them. "Gareth, Kelvan, this is my mother, Adora."

Adora surprised them all by bowing low to Kelvan in the old way first, before she even acknowledged his rider. The dragon preened openly at the show of respect and stood to his full height, returning the courtesy with a formal sweep of his wings.

"You honor my humble home with your presence, Sir Kelvan. Be welcome here."

"The honor is mine, Madam. Your daughter claimed you once knew one of my kind and I am pleased to see the old ways preserved in your memory. You do both our peoples proud." Kelvan included them all in his silent speech.

Adora blushed prettily as she straightened. "You are a handsome dragon, Sir Kelvan, and a pretty talker."

The dragon rumbled in a way resembling laughter and all the humans smiled as he laid the dead stag at the lady's feet.

"An offering for your table, madam. Courtesy of your daughter."

"And Kelvan too, Mama. That's how we met. I shot the stag, but he didn't see me and snagged it from above for a snack. I disputed his claim to the stag and he brought me to Gareth to see who was in the right."

"Ah yes, you bring me not only a dragon, but a knight as well." Adora clapped her hands together in joy, though her tone was mischievous. "You are Sir Gareth?"

The young man strode forward to stand before her. "I am."

"Welcome to our home, sir. It has been many years since I last saw a dragon and I must admit complete ignorance of the knights who work with them. The dragon I knew as a child had no partner at the time."

Gareth smiled kindly down at her. He was very tall and built on a large, sturdy frame.

"We are not much different from normal men, Lady, except that we can hear the dragons as you do and partner with them to protect the innocent."

"It is a noble calling," Adora replied. She liked the look of this knight, though his presence portended danger to her home...and perhaps to her daughter.

Gareth inclined his head to acknowledge her words. He was very polite and well spoken.

Adora continued her train of thought. "Your being here is worrisome, though. If you are here in my forest, trouble must not be far behind."

"You are perceptive, madam." The dragon's powerful voice sounded through all their minds. "Trouble brews on the border and the king has dispatched us to create a new Lair not far from here. You must be cautious in your travels and dealings with strangers. The skiths are growing restless."

Adora gasped but did not otherwise show the fear his stark words brought to her soul. She thought through the dire news as she made her guests welcome and turned the subject to more pleasant matters. At least on the surface.

She asked them about the new Lair they were building and prepared refreshments while Kelvan, in an uncharacteristically thoughtful move for a dragon, dragged the stag away into the forest to prepare it for the women. A few strategic swipes with his razor-sharp talons, and the meat was dressed and ready for cooking.

When he came back, they were sitting around the outdoor fire pit in front of the small cottage, talking amiably. Being certain he had everyone's attention, Kelvan covered one nostril with an overly large digit and exhaled a burst of flame over the meat. When the flame subsided, it was fully cooked, just right for human consumption.

"Dinner is served."

They all laughed and Adora passed around plates and utensils while Gareth carved and served each in turn. She also served drink and some of the tubers she'd been preparing before they arrived. It worked well as a side dish to the feast of meat.

Kelvan had already eaten, but he'd saved a few raw tidbits to nibble on while the humans ate. He was surprisingly neat for such a large beast and he reminded Adora again of the dragon she'd known as a child.

They talked of general things. The building of the new Lair and how far it was from the village. Gareth talked a little about the areas they would be patrolling and the warning systems they were setting up. Adora found it fascinating. And disturbing.

After dinner, Gareth and Belora took a walk down to the stream to gather water and steal a few moments alone together. It was growing increasingly obvious to Adora that her beautiful daughter was deeply in love, as was the tall young man at her side.

His heart was in his eyes as he looked down at her girl, and she knew it was a long-lasting kind of love that filled his heart. Though she had never known a knight before, she knew dragons. Her childhood dragon friend had taught her that the men they chose to fight with had the highest qualities of nobility and honor. She had little to worry about as far as her daughter's match was concerned, but still her heart grew heavy watching them.

"He loves true and deep, milady. It's the nature of knights to decide what they want quickly and pursue it with all haste. Many recognize their life mates within moments of meeting. The Mother of All guides them in every facet of their lives. Fear not for your daughter." The dragon settled across from Adora by the fire, his wings folded loosely against his sides as he reclined.

"I fear not for her, though I thank you for your words of comfort. If anything, I fear for my own future, selfish as it seems." Adora shook herself and changed the subject before the dragon had a chance to ask questions. "It's not important. Belora told you I knew a dragon when I was a child. I used to bring her melons from our garden and she would always slice a little piece for me as a treat. You remind me of her, Sir Kelvan. You have similar coloring in your wings and around your eyes. Her name was Kelzy." She sighed, lost in memory. "She had a scar running near her left ear."

"And another on her right foreleg."

"Yes! How did you know?"

Kelvan bowed his head to the side. *"She is my mother."* His voice was solemn. *"And you are Adora. She speaks of you often."*

Adora was pretty sure nobody had mentioned her given name to the dragon. He'd been calling her *milady* all evening, as had his knight. That he knew it shocked her. It also helped prove his claim.

"Kelzy lives still?" A smile bloomed on her pretty face. That the dragon friend of her youth might still be alive brought joy to her heart.

Kelvan chuckled softly in his dragonish way. *"Our kind does not age as you do. When you knew her, she had suffered the loss of her knight and needed time to recover. We bond very closely to our partners. My mother is one of the elders in charge of building our new Lair and she teaches the younger ranks how to fight and work with their knights. She chose my knight for me, in fact, even before I could claim him."*

"She chose well." Adora's eyes followed the progress of the young couple across the small clearing. They were strolling slowly, oblivious to all except each other.

"He is a good man through and through. You have naught to fear for your daughter or yourself, Lady Adora."

"It is selfish of me, I know, but I fear being alone. I've already lost children and it nearly killed me. Still, I want my baby to be happy, and her happiness lies with the young knight. It's obvious to see."

"Then come with us to the new Lair. I am certain my mother would welcome you."

"I refuse to be a burden. This is Bel's time. I don't want to interfere."

"You would not be a burden, Lady Adora. We always need help in the Lair, and there are so few humans able to deal well with my kind. We already know you and your daughter can. We would welcome you both. And you would be safe there."

Adora considered his words carefully, mulling over the possibilities in her mind. "I can cook and clean, I suppose. I also know of healing herbs. It's how I've made a living out here in the forest."

"Healing skills are always needed among the fighters. You would be more than welcome, Lady. What can it hurt to come for a visit? I know my mother will want to see you. If you do not come back with us, at least for a visit, I can nearly guarantee she will make the trip out here herself to make certain you are all right. She is not a young dragon any longer. Won't you spare her such an arduous journey? I can have you there and back again in the next day, if you will consent to come for a visit."

Adora was torn, but she did so want to see the dragon who had been her childhood friend once more. "Perhaps a short visit. Just to see Lady Kelzy. I have thought of her often and missed her greatly. But I must return to care for my patients. I am all the help the local village has, and I can't just abandon them."

"Yet you do not live in the village." His tone was quizzical.

"By choice. Not because they would not have us. When I came here, I was hurt deeply by the loss of my children. Twin girls as bright as the sun." She paused while she collected herself. Her baby girls were gone and it left a hole in her heart that was wide and deep. How she missed them still, years later. Nothing would ever make up for losing her beloved twin daughters. The only consolation she had was that Belora was still with her, still safe. She sighed deeply before continuing. "I couldn't bear to be with other people, and my work often brings me into the forest to gather herbs. I enjoy the solitude and don't have much. This place was empty and available. It needed a good cleaning and still needs some repair, but it's home. It welcomed me, helped me heal, and sheltered Bel as she grew. This place has been good to me."

Kelvan bowed his head in respect. *"I can feel the love in your words for this place. Our new Lair begins to feel that way to me as well, though I've only been there a short time. Perhaps because my mother was able to set it up to her specifications it has always felt like home. I have come to learn that home is wherever those you love are, so for me, home will always be with Gareth and his mate."*

"You think Belora is his mate?"

"I do. He moves slowly to claim her though, because she does not know our ways. I think that once she sees how we live and learns more about us, she'll fit in well. The Mother of All would not be so cruel as to bring them together only to break their hearts." They watched the two young people walking back from the stream, hand in hand. It was obvious how much in love the two were, though they had only met that day. *"You must come visit, Lady. It will help if you can see how your daughter will live and know that she is not gone from you forever. I'll fly her back to see you as often as possible if you choose to stay here after you've seen the Lair. I understand the importance of family."*

"You are a kind and noble being, Sir Kelvan." Adora reached up and placed her small palm on his knee joint. "I'll go with you to visit your new home and see Lady Kelzy once more. But only for a short time. With war coming, my duty is to the people of the village who depend on me."

"If you were male, you would surely have been a knight, Lady. Your heart is compassionate and strong."

"I think that's the most beautiful thing anyone has ever said to me." She smiled softly and turned back to watch the younger couple, kissing in the dappled moonlight, distantly in the forest. She thought they looked right together—her baby girl with a handsome and strong knight who so obviously cared for her. It was like a dream come true. For Belora.

Adora sighed wistfully, resigned to knowing that this time was for her daughter, but still it saddened her that she would never know such a love again. Her time was over.

Chapter Three

The dragon tried not to gloat as his mind sought out that of his partner. *"Lady Adora has agreed to come with us for a short visit to the Lair. She wants to see my mother, and I told her Kelzy was far too old and decrepit to fly all this way out to see her."*

Gareth burst into laughter and sent his thoughts back to the dragon as all knights were trained to do. *"Kelzy will singe your hide for even suggesting that she's too old to fly this short a distance. Your mother is one of our finest fighters, Kel, and by dragon reckoning, she's still quite young."*

"You know that and I know that, but Lady Adora doesn't. You should be thanking me for getting her to agree so easily to come along. These females belong at the Lair, Gareth. You know that as well as I do. We need them."

"You're right, Kel." Gareth sighed. *"I've only just met her, but I know in my heart, Belora is mine. And her mother seems a treasure. We don't have enough healers at our new Lair if it comes to war. There are so few women who can deal well with dragons and knights alike. We need every one."*

"These two are special. My mother saw the light in Adora as a child, so clearly that she still talks of her to this day. Belora is the same. If she consents to be your mate, you will be truly blessed."

"Don't you think you're getting a bit ahead of yourself? First we have to see if she can live at the Lair."

"But you want her."

"Of course I want her. But don't forget, she must choose me, Kel. Without her trust and her love, it will never work."

"The Mother of All would not put her in our path only to take her away. She is not so cruel."

Later, after a quick flight from Adora's house in the woods to the new Lair, Kelvan alighted on the ledge carved out from the stone face of the cliff for just that purpose. It was wide enough for several dragons to take off and land on at any one time and there was one already there, waiting for them.

"Kelzy." Adora whispered in a choked voice as she caught sight of the waiting blue-green dragon.

Belora squeezed her mother's hand and they shared a smile as Kelvan came to a complete stop. Gareth jumped down first, helping the women down. Adora strode directly to the waiting dragon and made a deep bow before her.

"Lady Kelzy, it is so good to see you again."

"Adora? Is it really you?" The huge dragon stepped closer, all formality forgotten as she lowered her head to the human's height. *"Adora, my child."* The dragon's voice was so gentle in her mind. *"Give us a hug, dear."*

The woman threw herself at the dragon, her arms wrapping tightly around her thick neck, weeping openly. The dragon did something then that dragons seldom did. She wrapped her great wings around the woman, encasing her in their magical warmth as Adora clung to her long lost childhood friend.

Kelzy knew she was overly emotional for a dragon and unusually fond of her human friends, but the little woman hugging her so tightly was the closest thing she had to a daughter. Kelzy had missed her terribly during those years they'd been separated. Finding her again so unexpectedly was a miracle.

"Mama Kelzy, I've missed you so," Adora whispered.

Kelzy crooned in her mind, soothing the woman's fears and basking in the joy of having the child of her heart near once more. She knew the others were watching them but didn't care. Kelzy had always been her own dragon and she didn't care for those that would comment on her uncharacteristic display. Adora was special. She always had been. Losing track of the small human girl had been one of the saddest things that had ever happened to Kelzy and finding her again was a gift from the Mother of All.

When Adora finally gathered her emotions and stepped back, Kelzy let her go with joy in her heart. Her gaze turned to her grown son and his partner. She did a double take when she spotted a younger human woman with the same light around her as Adora. This was Adora's child and, if she wasn't much mistaken, her light was already affecting the broad-shouldered knight at her side. Kelzy felt an extreme satisfaction. Her boy would have Adora's child as his partner's mate. It all suddenly made sense.

"You have a beautiful daughter," Kelzy told her. *"She will make a fine addition to our community."*

Adora reached back and motioned her daughter closer. "My daughter, Belora."

Belora made her bow prettily and said all the right words, impressing the dragon and no doubt making her mother proud.

"And where is your man?" Kelzy wanted to know. Surely the girl had a father lurking about somewhere. Kelzy wasn't certain any human man was worthy of her Adora, but she'd put up with him for her sake.

"I'm a widow. Have been for many years. We live simply, in the forest."

No mate was worse than a bad mate, and Kelzy didn't like the idea of Adora being all alone. She deserved happiness and a loving family of her own. Kelzy would fix that, if it was within her power.

"That will not do. You must stay here, with us. I have need of you, Adora. There is much work to be done and so few to do it."

"I—"

"Don't answer now. Come see how we live here and learn a bit of our ways and needs. Then, if you still feel like living all alone in your forest, I will take you back myself."

Adora smiled up at the dragon, love shining in her eyes, but started as she looked just past the dragon's tall shoulder. Kelzy turned her head to see what had startled her long lost daughter and puffed a small cloud of smoke in wry amusement.

"Don't let his looks frighten you, dear. This is Jared, my partner. Be nice, Jared, this girl is as a daughter to me." Kelzy was speaking to the minds of both humans, linking them just slightly.

Adora was startled by the feeling of the knight's curiosity. It reached her through the small, mental link formed by the dragon. She had never experienced such a thing before and it was surprising.

"I'm honored to meet you, Madam."

The knight's rich, baritone voice caught Adora off guard, warming her insides in a way they hadn't been warmed in too many years. The man was striking. Older than she, he had a jagged scar running down one cheek, all too close to his eye, though the silvery blue depths of his irises remained unhurt and stunningly alert. His hair was dark with light streaks of silver near his temples that only made him appear more dangerous somehow. She got the impression that this man seldom smiled but was competent and deadly in his chosen profession as a warrior.

A tall man, he was muscular in a lithe sort of way, but solid and all too handsome for his own good. The only relief was that he didn't seem to be aware of his rugged appeal, or if he was, he disdained such things in favor of more sober pursuits. He seemed very serious and almost grim, but Adora saw a sadness in his eyes that called to the sorrow in her own soul. Instinctively, her heart went out to him, though he gave no indication of wanting or needing any sort of sympathy or even camaraderie.

"The honor is mine, Sir Jared." Adora realized belatedly that she was staring rather rudely and made her curtsey quickly, averting her gaze to the ground while she felt her cheeks flame.

"Honestly, Jared, make an effort. You're frightening the poor child." Kelzy's teasing voice was just a bit exasperated in both of their minds and Adora had to stifle a giggle.

Jared was humbled by the woman's beauty. Her green eyes were luminous as she raised them once more to his. Though Kelzy insisted on referring to her as a girl, there was no doubt in his mind that this was a woman. She had the rounded curves he enjoyed and a sparkle in her eyes when she looked at him that set his teeth on edge.

He was a widower and the loss of his wife many years before had been hard on him. Since then, he had found pleasure where he could, but had no desire to marry again or become involved in anything remotely long-term.

But here was a woman who was already close to his dragon partner—the only female he allowed in his life. Undoubtedly Kelzy would want this woman nearby. Their relationship pre-dated his own with the dragon and was obviously as close, or perhaps even closer, than the relationship between he and Kelzy, bonded as they were. This woman would most likely be underfoot and he couldn't ignore her.

His heart didn't want to ignore her, and that's what unsettled him most. It had been a very long time indeed since a woman had such an impact on him. The echo of emotion he felt through the link with Kelzy when the dragon spoke to them both was the oddest phenomenon he had ever experienced.

He wondered idly if mated knights had this sort of non-verbal feedback through the link with their dragons. He hadn't been partnered with Kelzy during his marriage, so he had never experienced it for himself. In fact, it had been his wife's death that brought Kelzy to him. His pain had drawn the dragon from her own sorrow over the loss of her first knight partner and they had bonded as they helped each other through the emotional upheaval of losing someone they loved.

"Kelzy has told me many stories about you as a child. I know she missed you greatly." He remembered his manners with a little nudge from the flat of Kelzy's sharp front talon against his calf.

"No more than I missed her."

The woman glowed. There was no other word for it. Her goodness and light shone in her eyes and around her curved womanly body in a way that made him want to move closer.

"Adora, you will stay in our suite. It is quite obvious my son's knight and your girl wish to be alone together." Kelzy's satisfied tone had both Adora and Jared looking back at Gareth and Belora, who were currently locked at the lips. *"We have plenty of room and I suspect we'll talk long into the night. I want to know everything that's happened to you since last we saw each other. And I want to know all about your daughter too, since I have little doubt she will soon be part of my son's human family."*

The woman's soft gaze went from her little girl, to Kelzy, then to Jared. He knew she waited for him to second the invitation, since it was his suite too. Jared could do no less than step forward, even though his internal alarms warned him about getting too involved. This soft woman could well break what little was left of his heart.

"You should stay with us. There's plenty of room, as Kelzy says."

He thought he detected relief and a spark of interest in her expression, but dared not read too much into it. He was a confirmed bachelor now. He didn't need love in his life. It made him soft. It made him weak. It made him hurt.

Kelzy was the only female he needed. At least she wasn't likely to die and leave him alone and in pain.

"Thank you," Adora answered softly. "I'd be honored to stay with you."

Her answer made his heart skip a beat, no matter how hard he tried not to let it.

"Let's leave them for a bit," Kelzy suggested. *"We have so many years to catch up on."*

They left the younger couple and headed for Kelzy's suite. Jared escorted her, though it was obvious to Adora that he was careful to maintain a certain distance. The man alarmed her a bit, but she thought there was a deep sensitivity in him and her sixth sense about people was seldom wrong. This man had been hurt badly in his life and the gruff exterior was probably all for show. Besides, she reasoned, Mama Kelzy was an excellent judge of character and the dragon chose the knight, not the other way around.

Adora was amazed to learn that the dragons had warm sand pits in their suites heated from below somehow. Their human partners had built rooms for themselves around the sand wallows. Each single dragon or mated dragon pair had their own wallow which was divided from the rest of the Lair by a ring of rooms that made up their suite. The knights and their mate would live in the suite with their dragons, some having guest rooms attached as well as utility and storage rooms.

The arrangement appeared quite cozy and served both the knights and their dragon partners well, but Adora noticed quickly, as they walked through the halls, that there were far fewer women in the Lair than men. The dragons seemed to be about fifty percent female and fifty percent male and all partnered with male knights, but there were few mated dragons and only those mated pairs seemed to have mated knights.

Adora intended to ask about it, but all the wondrous things she was learning and seeing for the first time quickly sidetracked her. As they passed a huge steaming chamber, Jared told her the pools within were heated, as the wallows were, from the earth beneath, and the water had a fragrant mineral quality she had never before encountered.

Since it was already past time for the evening meal, Jared volunteered to go to the kitchens and bring something back for Adora while she freshened up from the flight. Kelzy sat down for a good roll in her heated sand wallow and both females were content for the moment.

An hour later, Jared found Adora, now changed out of her traveling clothes and wearing a simple nightgown, cuddled up under Kelzy's wing. She slept soundly in the dragon's warm wallow with her.

It was unheard of. Shocking. Yet somehow it softened his heart to see this strong woman tucked up like a child against the side of the kindest dragon Jared had ever known.

"Don't wake her." Kelzy said softly in his mind. *"She's had a hard time of it."*

"You really weren't kidding when you said she was like a daughter to you, were you?" Jared spoke mind to mind with Kelzy to avoid making noise that might wake the small woman sleeping so peacefully next to the huge dragon.

"She could be no closer to my heart if she were a dragonet. This girl has the purest heart of any human I've ever known. Don't you see the light from her soul? It's in everything she touches, in all that she does. The Mother of All had blessed her as a child and I'm gratified to see that her heart has never wavered. It's as pure today as it was when she was little."

"Her daughter has that glow too," he agreed absently as he watched the small woman sleep.

"Then you do see it! I knew you, of all the knights here, would." Kelzy reached out with one smooth talon and touched his booted foot gently. She was very demonstrative for a dragon and often shocked the others with her displays of emotion. Jared shuddered to think what the others would say if they saw her sharing her wallow with a human. There had already been talk about her allowing the human to hug her.

"She's special, Jared. You must help me convince her to come live here with us. We need her. The Lair needs her and her daughter or the Mother of All would not have put them in my son's path."

"I will, of course, help in whatever way I can, Kelzy, but you should know I'm not looking for a wife."

"Did I say anything about you marrying her? Honestly, Jared. What makes you think I'd even think you were good enough for her? I won't let my girl consort with just any knight. So you'd better warn off your lusty friends."

"Methinks you protest a bit too much, Kelz." Jared had to stifle a chuckle as he walked away from the odd pair snuggled in the warm sand.

Belora watched with interest as Kelvan strode into the large chamber, heading straight for the pit of warm sand at its center. With obvious enjoyment, he kicked up a little cloud of sand as he settled in for a good roll and made dragonish purrs of contentment as the warm, dry sand rubbed against his scales, polishing them to a brilliant shine.

The setup of the knight's quarters intrigued Belora. Everything was built around Kelvan's oval wallow. A small room for eating and preparing meals sat off to one side with sealed containers of what looked like beer keeping cold in the trickle of water down the side of the stone wall. She went over to investigate and realized that by removing a small trap, the flow of water could be increased or decreased to nothing at all. A large stone basin lay beneath with a drain that led off somewhere below, presumably down farther into the mountain from which this Lair was carved.

"Magic," she breathed, removing the trap to watch the flow of icy clear water.

"And a good dose of science as well." Gareth chuckled as he leaned back against the doorframe, watching her. "His Majesty sent a mage to help us redirect the energies of the earth so we could heat our baths and the dragons' wallows, but he also sent a skilled architect who could direct the flow of water for washing and drinking. The two worked hand in hand to design this place for both humans and dragons to live comfortably."

"It's a marvel."

"You haven't seen all of it yet." Gareth held out his hand to her. She took it and moved through the rooms with him. "Let me give you the tour of our quarters. You already saw Kelvan's wallow. The dragons' wallows are the centerpieces of each set of rooms though they vary in size according to location in the mountain, how many dragons need to live there and other factors. Since I am still unmated, Kelvan's wallow is sized for one dragon only."

"And a great hardship it is. I barely have room to turn around." A great flick of Kelvan's tail sent a shower of sand over the chuckling humans.

"I keep brooms on hand to sweep the sand back in the wallow each day, else I'd soon feel like I was living on a beach." He took one of the brooms leaning up against the circular wall and began sweeping the warm sand back into the pit.

"Better a beach than a hermitage."

"What does he mean?" Belora looked from Kelvan's smoky snort of disgust to Gareth's shaking head.

"My partner thinks I spend too much time alone." He pulled her close into his arms. "But I won't be alone tonight, will I?"

Belora giggled. She actually giggled. She was shocked such a flirty, feminine sound came out of her body, but there it was. Something about this knight brought out the floozy in her, but it felt good. Freeing.

"No, you won't be alone tonight, Gareth." Blushing, she reached for his hand. "Why don't you show me your room? And your bed."

"All in good time." He patted her hand. "But I bet you're still too sore to really test the bed yet. Not to worry, I have a solution." He pulled aside a screen that hid the entrance to a small bathing chamber. It had a stone tub sunk partially into the floor and another of those trap devices that Gareth pulled to allow water to trickle into the tub in a steady rhythm.

"This water is from the mineral springs. By the time it makes its way here from there it's little more than lukewarm but we have Kel to help us warm it again, if we ask him nicely. A hot soak in the healing mineral water and a little dragon magic will put you right again in no time."

"Dragon magic?" She turned to watch the dragon. He craned his neck out of the sand pit and up onto the warm stone floor so that his great head rested only a few feet away from the bathing tub. His jewel-like eyes settled on her unflinchingly. It was slightly unnerving.

"Didn't your mother tell you that the dragon's breath has

healing properties? I will gladly expend my energies to soothe your torn flesh if it means I can share in your pleasure again like this afternoon. I have never felt the like."

"You...you felt that?" Belora blushed to the roots of her hair, looking from dragon to knight and back again for some explanation.

"We bond closely with our knights. We're always present in each other's minds. We each feel what the other feels. It's our greatest strength and perhaps also our main weakness, but it is the way of things. When you joined with Gareth, I felt the echo of his pleasure and your own." His wide mouth opened in a toothy grin. *"It was marvelous."*

Embarrassed beyond belief, Belora didn't know what to think.

"Don't worry, sweet." Gareth took her in his arms as the tub filled behind him. There was a small stool just to the side at the foot of the tub and he led her to it. "It's the way of things for knights and their dragon partners. There's nothing to be ashamed of."

"I...I just didn't realize."

"I know." Gareth soothed her with his hands, undoing buttons as he stroked her shoulders and arms. "And I would have told you sooner, but we've been a bit busy today."

She chuckled. "To say the least."

"Now, how about that hot bath?" He reached out to close the water trap. "Kel, will you do the honors?"

"Gladly." Breathing deeply, the dragon aimed a wonderfully warm exhalation of hot air at the full tub, heating the chamber and the water as easy as that. He returned his head to its reclining position at the foot of the tub, watching the humans lazily.

"Is he going to watch? I can't... um... take off my clothes in front of him." She blushed again, unreasonable bashfulness taking over her mind.

"Why not? You are a beautiful woman, but even if you weren't, I'm a dragon. Not human."

"But..."

"Your modesty is misplaced. I'll feel everything Gareth feels, even know what you're feeling through my link with you both. I couldn't be any more present if I were human and could fuck you myself." She gasped, but he forged ahead. *"Won't you let me enjoy what little pleasure I can gain from this? Until Gareth officially claims his mate, I cannot claim my own dragoness. It's strictly forbidden, and for good reason."*

"Is that true?"

Gareth nodded. "Just as he feels my passion, I'll feel his. Dragon mating is, from what I've been told, overpowering to humans. Unless I have a mate to be with during his mating flights, it would drive me mad. Even among mates, sometimes the humans get into a frenzy that can be dangerous."

"Oh, my." She turned compassionate eyes to the dragon lolling in the huge archway. "So you've never..."

He stirred himself to shake his head sadly. *"Until Gareth mates, I cannot."*

Belora walked slowly over to the dragon, feeling both sets of male eyes trained on her as she moved unexpectedly. She knelt down by Kel's massive head and leaned forward to kiss the ridge just between his eyes.

"You are a good and noble creature, Sir Kelvan. I'm sorry to have doubted you."

With a nod, she stood and removed all her clothing, standing before the dragon as if for inspection as he sighed out a warm puff of air that tickled her. She laughed and turned toward Gareth, who had shed his own clothing. He reached for her, and together they slid into the warm bath, locked at the lips as if they hadn't kissed in years rather than mere minutes.

The water lulled her and when a long, hot tongue dipped into the water and circled her ankle, she squealed. Apparently the dragon wanted to participate. She lifted her leg as he tugged upward, then allowed him to do the same to her other leg, draping both over the lips of the massive tub on either side. She was spread before him, Gareth to her side, watching now as the dragon's head loomed over the tub.

"What's he doing?" The nervous edge was back in her voice.

"Healing you," Gareth whispered against her breast, just bobbing above the water. He licked her nipple and bit down as Kelvan breathed over them both. This time, the dragon's breath contained magic as well as heat. She'd never felt it before, but she knew the dragon magic resonated within her body— especially the sore parts.

She felt a healing fire of magic within her. This was dragon energy, exciting even as it healed. She had almost come from having a dragon heal her. Could things get any weirder?

Apparently they could. When Gareth lifted her from the tub long moments later after washing every square inch of her body—some twice and three times—he spread her out on the warm stone floor near Kelvan's massive head.

"Just one more thing to be certain you'll feel no pain from what we do together." Gareth looked up at Kelvan and spread her thighs far apart, holding them there and spreading her wide with his hands. "Kel?"

"My pleasure."

The dragon rumbled and brought forth an even thicker dose of the vapor she'd come to realize was the magical dragon's breath. Everywhere the misty cloud of sweet, cinnamon-scented smoke enveloped her, she felt the warmth of healing magic. The dragon's breath was very, very special. Kelvan must have expended a great deal of his energy to put forth such potent magic.

She felt euphoric as the mist faded, her skin tingling with the touch of healing and her body raring to go. It felt as if the long afternoon of loving had taken no toll whatsoever on her untried body, and she knew it was all because of Kelvan and his willingness to expend his precious magical energy on her wellbeing.

She scrambled onto her knees and went over to him, uncaring of her nudity now. What a difference a few minutes can make, she realized in one small part of her mind that worried over such things.

"May I touch you?" she asked formally. She hadn't asked before and realized her lapse in manners. This time, the dragon didn't see her coming. His eyes were closed in fatigue and his head and long neck lolled heavily on the stone of the floor while the rest of his body relaxed in the sand pit.

Kelvan rolled his head to one side and stared at her as if considering her request. Slowly, he blinked his agreement and she moved forward to place her hands on the ridges just below his enormous eyes. Holding his jeweled gaze, she focused her own small power and sent what healing magic she could back to him the way her mother had taught her. His eyes widened as Gareth stood abruptly to watch.

"You are a healer? A true healer?"

Belora shrugged and sat back. "I have only a small gift when compared with my mother, but as you know, healers cannot usually heal themselves. Thank you for expending your energy for me, Sir Kelvan. I hope I have returned at least a bit of what you gave me."

"More than I gave, if truth be known. You have more of a gift than you realize. Your energy has the flavor of dragons."

She yawned and shrugged. "If you say so." She was tired now, where before she'd been nearly bursting with the dragon's energy, but it was a normal sort of fatigue. One earned by a long day. It was how she would have felt if not for the dragon's magical intervention, and she was pleased to know she'd given him back the massive energy boost he'd inadvertently transferred to her while healing.

"It's time for bed." Gareth scooped her up in his arms and carried her into the sleeping chamber. All the arched doorways in the large suite of rooms were wide so Kelvan could lay his head down right in the middle of them. His head, craning on that long, sinuous neck, followed them right into the bedchamber. He came to rest opposite the pile of sumptuous furs and stuffed pillows that was Gareth's bed. Belora had never been in such a luxurious resting place. She stretched and smiled as she felt Gareth come up beside her, his hands roving over her still-tingling body.

"I hope you're not too tired to make love."

"I don't think I'll ever be too tired to make love with you, Gareth. You make me feel so alive."

Chapter Four

Gareth looked from the dragon in his doorway to the gorgeous woman lying in his bed and realized he had never been more content. Right here he had everything he would ever need in life. His dragon partner had been the main focus of his life for so long, he had not quite realized how a mate would complete the circle. Yet Belora's presence in his room, in his bed, in his heart, made him see things in a whole new light.

She was the woman for him. Of that he had no doubt. Now he only need convince her of it and gentle her to their ways. Life in a dragon's Lair was odd to most humans but necessary to the nature of both the dragons and their human partners. He prayed to the Mother of All that Belora would be able to accept their ways. No doubt they were hardest on the woman involved, but the benefits were great. The old adage held true in this case—the greatest prize often demanded the greatest sacrifice.

Gently he lay down next to Belora, touching her softly, knowing she welcomed his touch, his love. It was a heady feeling. Slowly he lowered his head to her body, licking the mineral saltiness of their bathwater from her dewy skin.

"What you do to me, Gareth. I never knew..."

He sucked her nipple into his mouth and she gasped, unable to complete her thoughts. He kept at it until she was shivering, moving on the bed sensuously. A puff of warm air from the doorway had her lifting her head to meet the jeweled gaze of the dragon, watching them.

"To warm you, Mistress. You looked cold."

She giggled. "I wasn't cold, Kelvan, and well you know it."

Gareth lifted above her, blocking her view of the dragon.

"You don't mind that he's here? Truly?"

She tilted her head as if considering. "It still seems a little strange, but it's all right. I mean, it's not like he's human, after all."

"How would you feel if he were?" Gareth's eyes darkened.

"You mean having another man watch us?" She shivered against him and the look in her eyes was not one of fear as she mulled over his words. Her reaction gave him hope. "I don't know. That seems stranger still. I was a virgin until I met you, Gareth. Give me some time to adjust."

"I know I'm rushing things, sweet. Just kick me if I go too fast, okay?" He leaned down and kissed her. "But having you here in my bed makes me think of all sorts of strange notions." He nibbled on her neck, working his way down her body as she squirmed in pleasure. "And for the record, being watched doesn't bother me. Quite the opposite, in fact. To have other men able to see what belongs to me—what they'll never have—it's a tantalizing thought."

She wiggled again as he spread her legs with his hands and settled between them. He gazed at her for a long while, slowly threading his fingers through the neat hair at the juncture of her thighs before spreading the outer lips of her pussy and touching within.

He knew that together, he and Kelvan had healed the worst of her injury, but still he did his best to be extra gentle. He would die rather than hurt this special woman, the other half of his heart. He leaned forward and swirled his tongue through her folds, then moved it right up into her channel as she cried out in pleasure.

Belora came almost at once as the dragon puffed warm air over them and rumbled low in his throat. Gareth stayed with her through the orgasm, stroking her ever higher with his tongue and questing fingers. He brought her wetness down to the tiny hole of her rear and probed gently within, setting off another series of visible shockwaves.

"You like that?" he breathed against her skin.

She moaned in pleasure as he continued teasing her. When he judged she was ready, he sat back, flipping her over and massaging the rounded cheeks of her ass.

"Get on your hands and knees, pet."

She looked back at him, uncertain, but his playful slap to her ass made her squeal and move. The spank had not really hurt. He'd meant it only to tease. The widening of her eyes and her panting breaths told him all he needed to know about her reaction to it. She moved to her hands and knees uncertainly, but he soothed her, parting the cheeks of her ass with gentle fingers.

When he could hold back no longer, he moved behind her and brought his cock to the entrance of her dripping pussy. She was beyond excited. She was primed. Pushing in, he went slow as she moaned.

"It feels so much bigger this way." Her gasping words reached his ears and brought a satisfied smile to his face.

"Too big?" He teased by stopping about halfway in.

"No!" She moved back against him, trying to take him deeper. "It feels good! Don't stop."

He chuckled and moved forward again, seating himself fully. He stayed there for a moment, savoring the sensation until his needs grew fierce once again and he started to move. She was moaning beneath him and he used his hands to steady her, playing with the little hole of her anus and teasing her response.

She jerked and cried out as his finger dipped into her ass, just to the first knuckle. He kept it there, noting her reactions as his pace increased. He was close now and she was downright explosive beneath him.

When he was on the edge of orgasm, he pushed his finger in deeper, at the same time reaching around to tease her clit with his other hand. She came like fireworks, clenching around him and milking his cock until he shuddered and cried out, jetting his seed deep within her.

They collapsed together onto the pile of bedding and he folded her gently into his arms. Drifting off to sleep, he realized he had never reached a higher plateau of pleasure in his life, and never would again with any other woman. Belora was it for him. His mate.

He smiled as sleep claimed him, knowing she was in his arms where she belonged.

Gareth woke in the night when Belora moved restlessly in her sleep. He wasn't used to sleeping with a woman, but waking with Belora in his arms was an entirely satisfying experience. He soothed her and she settled back against him. He looked around the room and found Kelvan's head still resting in the doorway, watching them.

"Gareth, there's something strange about her healing energy."

"Strange? Strange in a bad way?"

"No! It feels...it feels almost like...no, I must be wrong."

"Spit it out, Kel."

"No, I shouldn't say anything unless I'm sure. Let me think on this a bit more, but by all means, don't let her go back to that hut in the forest. If I'm right, she is more precious than you know."

"Go to sleep, Kel. We can puzzle out your cryptic words tomorrow." Gareth threw a pillow at the dragon and cuddled

closer to his woman. Everything would work out now that they were together. He could feel it.

The next morning, after a small meal in the communal area where both Belora and her mother were introduced to most of those who lived in the Lair, Gareth and Kelvan went off to train. As one of the younger and less experienced pairs, they would not be excused from training lightly. Likewise, Jared and Kelzy had important matters to attend to in setting up the new Lair. They deposited Adora with her daughter and took off to their own work.

Left to their own devices, they made friends with a few of the women, but it was Silla, a woman about her mother's age that really took them under her wing. When both Belora and her mother volunteered to help with the daily chores, it was Silla who showed them where to go and what to do to help. Belora joined the small washing crew while her mother went off with the Lair's healer to discuss what might be needed in the stillroom.

It was almost dark when Kelvan alighted on the ledge outside the suite where Belora waited for them. She beamed when Gareth walked in. He felt more than a bit ragged beside his dragon partner, but she didn't seem to notice.

"Did you have a good day?" He wrapped her in his arms and kissed her.

"Wonderful, actually. The others are so friendly, and the dragons! They are just amazing. I think I could live here forever and never become bored."

Belora's smiling face enchanted him as she pulled away from him to fold the last of the linens. He'd told her to relax and enjoy her time here while he trained, but she'd insisted on pitching in when they had discussed it that morning. He admired her spirit and her giving heart, but he also wanted to pamper her. After seeing her house in the forest, he knew she hadn't led an easy life.

He wanted to make her life easier. He wanted to spoil her and shower her with love, attention, and all the material things she had never had before, but he knew her innate goodness wouldn't let her rest idle while others worked, and now he was glad of it. Working alongside the other women today had been a good thing, he realized, because it showed her how her life could be if she chose to stay with him in the Border Lair. He grabbed her by the waist and twirled her around, unable to contain the joy he felt at her unguarded words.

"Gareth! Put me down!"

He did, but then knelt at her feet, smiling up at her. "You have no idea the joy that fills me to hear you speak of my home in such a way."

"You must know how special this place is."

"I do. But even more special, is you, Belora, my beloved."

"Why are you kneeling?" She tried to tug his arms up, but he would not budge.

"It's tradition for a knight to humble himself before the woman he chooses when he asks the most important question he will ever ask of her."

She gasped. "What question is that?"

He tugged both of her soft hands into his and stared up into her eyes. "I love you, Belora. Will you be my wife?"

She gaped at him. She seemed hardly able to speak, but the smile that spread across her soft lips was answer in itself. "Yes, Gareth. I love you too!"

He drew her into his arms and kissed her hard, hugging

her tight and lifting her off the ground with his eagerness. He moved her to the bedroom and lay her down on the soft furs, kissing every inch of her body as he undressed her. He made short work of his own clothing and soon they were skin to skin. *The way it should always be,* he thought.

He rose above her and took her legs in his hands, caressing them before placing one on either side of his body. He knew what he wanted and couldn't wait. He tested her readiness with one hand before smiling in deep satisfaction. She was wet and more than ready.

"Take me, beloved. Squeeze me with your beautiful body and bring me pleasure like I've never known."

He entered her slowly, careful lest he hurt her, but once seated he groaned in bliss. His eyes squeezed shut for a moment as he savored the feeling of her warm body around him. When he opened his eyes and looked down into hers, he saw the tears there and stilled in panic.

"Did I hurt you?" He moved to lever himself off of her, but she surprised him by wrapping her legs around his waist and holding on tight.

"You could never hurt me, Gareth." Her whispered voice was full of wonder and her watery eyes shone with happiness. He began to relax and settled back onto her though he was curious about her reaction. "I'm just a little overwhelmed, I guess, by the beauty of this—of you. I love you so much."

The glow of her words pierced his heart. "As I love you, Belora. Never doubt that."

"I want to stay with you forever."

He began to move inside her, unable to hold back any longer.

"I want you too, Belora. For always and ever." He moved more urgently then, his mind blocking out the reality that she still didn't know all that would be expected of her as his mate, but he would deal with that later. It was enough for now to know that she wanted him and would accept him as her mate. The rest would come later.

He pounded home, again and again, bringing her to repeated peaks. She climaxed almost continuously under him while he steadily increased his pace, altering his position slightly to reach deeper or differently each time she came down from a yet higher peak. He played her body, manipulating her senses to bring her the most pleasure he knew how to give. When she finally sobbed at the highest climax yet, he knew he could hold out no longer.

With a harsh groan, he increased yet again, bringing her to the final, mind-blowing climax in which he joined her. He came for what seemed like hours, deep within the woman he loved. Potent and powerful, his climax wrung him out from deep within his soul while Belora shattered and shook with her own orgasm around him.

It went on for a blissfully long time and when it was over, he was completely drained. He had only enough energy to roll off her, pull the covers up over them both and tuck her into his arms securely before falling into the deepest, most peaceful sleep he'd known in years.

All was right with the world. Belora loved him and wanted to be with him. Life could hardly get better than this.

"So you have claimed your mate. You know what this means, don't you?" Kelvan's voice sounded through Gareth's mind the next day, lower than usual and more excited. Kelvan looked over at his partner with a curious tilt to his head. *"Now that you have found your mate, I am free to take mine."*

"You already have a female in mind?"

"I do." The dragon's rumble sounded suspiciously gruff.

"This sounds serious. Have you waited long to claim your lady love, Kelvan? Truly, I had no idea I was holding you up." Gareth was only half teasing.

"You know it's not safe for a fighting dragon to mate before his human partner. I knew you would find your mate sooner rather than later and I think I have exhibited extraordinary patience with you. Of course, as it turned out, I even had to find your mate for you to speed things along."

"That you did, my friend, and I'll thank you every day for it as long as I live." Gareth watched his little mate a few yards distant, moving gracefully in her way. She literally took his breath away. To think, she was his and his alone—at least until Kelvan took his mate. Then they would probably expand their circle of love to include Kelvan's mate and her partner. "So who is your lady?"

"And more importantly who is her partner, right?" Kelvan supplied with some humor. *"Don't worry, Gareth. We dragons take all into consideration when we choose our partners and mates. The Mother of All has no little influence in it either. Seldom has there been an incompatible partnering among our kind. You know this to be true."*

"Yes, but I still worry about exactly who I'm expected to share my mate with." Gareth's skin itched to think of the possibilities. He'd never had to confront the reality of mating among dragonkind before and had never really considered the problems it could cause to their human partners. He began to sweat as he thought of what would come when Kelvan finally took his mate. It could be glorious. Or it could be disastrous.

"You will be pleased then, I think, to learn that my mate is Rohtina."

A huge grin spread across Gareth's face. "And Lars is her partner. Kel, this couldn't have worked out better!"

The dragon dipped his great head. *"The Mother of All knows what She is about after all."*

"That She does."

A speculative gleam entered his eye. He and Lars were close. He knew and trusted the man and they worked well together. When their dragons mated, they would become part of a fighting unit, partners that would share everything—including the pleasure their dragons found in each other with the sole human female among the tightly knit group.

If Gareth had to pick a man to bring pleasure to his beloved mate, he could not have chosen better himself. Lars was a good man and he would love Belora as much as Gareth did. He would also help Gareth give her the greatest sexual pleasure a human woman could know. The dragons would see to it.

"Jared, will you talk some sense into her? She insists she's only here for a visit, but she must stay. Make her realize how much we need her." Kelzy's voice was tinged with frustration when Jared walked into their apartments to find the two females squared off in full argument mode. He had forgotten just how much females could squabble over inconsequential things.

"We cannot just commandeer the woman, Kelzy. She has her own life and must make her own decisions."

"Thank you, Sir Jared." Adora turned the full power of her gaze on him and he looked away uncomfortably. The woman seemed to see right through him with her pale, healer's gaze and it was jarring to say the least. "As I've told Mama Kelzy, I have responsibilities to the villagers. I'm their only source of medical help and they depend on me. I can't just abandon them."

"Why do you call her that?"

"What?" Adora seemed confused for a moment as she tilted her head up at him, her beautiful green eyes frowning.

"You call a dragon 'mama.' Didn't you realize? It's a bit odd, to say the least, but then Kelzy's always been a little overly demonstrative with humans, or so her fellow dragons would criticize."

"They're just busybodies. Who I consort with as friends and family is none of their business, dragon, human or otherwise."

"I didn't realize I still called you that, Lady Kelzy. I'm sorry." Adora's blushing cheeks spoke of her embarrassment.

"Now see what you've done, Jared? Sweetheart, you don't have to use titles with me. You are the daughter of my heart. It warms my soul to know you still think of me as your surrogate mother."

Kelzy stepped forward and Adora reached her hand out to stroke the dragon's tough, jewel-toned hide. The two females so obviously cared for one another.

"When I was very little, I got lost in the woods and stumbled into Kelzy's cave. I could barely speak, but I knew the word 'mama'. Kelzy returned me to my family, who were searching frantically through the woods. I know they were frightened to see her, but when they saw me on her back, smiling away and calling her mama, they knew I was safe. She deposited me back with my mother and father and after that they let me go see her whenever I wanted. She raised me as much as my parents did, watching out for me when I ventured into the woods."

"None of them could hear me or speak with me, but Adora had the strongest gift I have ever encountered. They may have raised you, but they were not your blood kin."

"What?"

"I never told you this because I didn't think it my place back then, but it was obvious to me that your mother and father were not your birth parents. They adopted you. If they had been your blood kin, at least one of them would have been able to

communicate with me. It's an inherited trait, passed down through the bloodlines, usually on the father's side. The man you called father had no such ability nor did any of your siblings. Your brothers, at least, should have been able to hear me if you shared the same parents."

"Then who are my parents?" Adora's voice trembled just a bit and her wide eyes looked shaken and a little lost.

"I couldn't say and for that I'm sorry. I often thought to go on a quest to see where you came from. After all, females with the dragon gift are rare and we need every one we can find. Especially with war coming."

"Then war is definitely on the way?" Adora's eyes darkened with worry.

"Yes." It was Jared who answered, his voice firm. "There's no escaping it now. The Skithdronian king has been working toward all-out war for a long time and he's just about ready now, we think, to launch it."

"Which is why you must stay here with us, Adora. You will have no protection in the forest. The skiths will ravage man and beast alike when they are loosed."

"Which is why I *must* go back. I'm the only healer within twenty leagues. I can't just abandon those people."

"We're flying patrols now. When the skiths come, we'll engage them whenever and wherever we find them." Jared kept his voice calm and deadly. He surprised even himself with the sentiments he was feeling. "We're here to protect the people and lands. What good can one unprotected healer do out there? Wouldn't your talents be better used here?"

"You may very well be right, Sir Jared, but I have to go back. They depend on me. I'm not so conceited as to think that my destiny lies in such a grand place. I'm a simple healer, not one to be worthy of working with your knights."

"Sheep dung! That is the most ridiculous thing I've ever

71

heard you say, Adora. And here I thought you were smart for a human."

Adora smiled softly. "I love you too, Mama Kelzy, but the fact remains, I must return to my cottage."

"Cottage? My son tells me it was no more than a hut! How can I leave you in such a place?"

Adora stroked the dragon's shiny scales soothingly. "Because you must. It's what I have to do."

"But you'll at least stay for your daughter's wedding, won't you?" Jared surprised himself by asking.

She nodded. "I'll stay for the mating feast, but I must go home the next day."

Kelzy snorted smoke, clearly upset. *"We will take you then, but don't expect me to be happy about it."*

"Kel will seek his mate soon." Gareth knew he had to tread lightly. Belora had not been raised in the Lair and did not know the way of things in dragon matings.

"He's already chosen a mate?" Belora spoke softly, wrapped in his arms in the dark of the night.

"He hasn't made his formal declaration yet, but he will soon. That means we'll be adding to our family as well."

She turned to peer up at him in the darkness. "How so?"

"When dragons mate, their human partners cannot help but share in the event. It's because of the close bond we share with our dragon partners. Kelvan intends to mate with Rohtina. Her partner is named Lars. He and I have been friends for a very long time. When Kel claims his mate, we will become family. Lars and I will train with our dragon partners and will go into battle together from then on. We will patrol together and work together—even live together in the same set of apartments."

"Does this Lars have a wife?"

Gareth shook his head. "No. There are so few women born with ability to hear the dragons, many of the knights never find a woman to share their lives. It was a miracle when Kelvan found you. He would have given you the stag, you know, but he made an issue out of it so he would be able to bring you to me. He suspected the Mother of All put you in our path so that I could find you and make you mine, and I quite agree."

"Praise the Mother, then. She certainly knows what She's doing." She reached up and kissed him deeply, caressing his cheek with her soft fingers.

"As soon as we move the rest of your things from your cabin into our new apartments, there will be a mating ceremony held for us. It's basically an excuse to eat, drink and be merry as our fellows wish us well. There will even be dancing."

"Gareth, I don't know how to dance." She sounded ashamed by her lack of skill, and it touched his heart. He'd give her everything and more, to make up for the things she'd missed in her life.

"Not to worry. I didn't expect you would know our style of dance anyway, so I talked to your mother and she's setting up some practice for us."

"What's different about your kind of dancing?"

He shifted uncomfortably. "Since there are so few women among us, our dances are designed around sets of three—two men and one woman. We don't dance often, but a mating ceremony is one of the times when tradition requires it, and it really is a lot of fun. Don't worry; you'll enjoy it. I promise."

Chapter Five

Lars was a big man, as tall as Gareth, but even more muscular. Where Gareth had the sleek muscles of a racehorse, Lars had a stockier sort of strength. His hair was the color of pale wheat and his eyes a sparkling turquoise that crinkled at the corners when he smiled. His smile, when it appeared, was open, generous and surprisingly kind, though it seemed he was a quiet man by nature.

Belora took one look at him and had to fight an odd feeling in the pit of her stomach. Was it right to be so attracted to a man after pledging your life to another? She wasn't sure, but she found it impossible not to notice the tingle in her skin when he took her hand in the moves of the dances they were teaching her. She caught his eyes twinkling at her with an odd sort of speculation and a definite masculine appreciation that nearly took her breath away.

She thought she intercepted pointed glances between the men that made her loins burn. When she caught Gareth's eye he was wholly approving of her, encouraging her to learn the more intricate steps of the progressively harder—and more intimate—dances they showed her. By the time they moved on to the "mating dance" that would culminate the feast in their honor, her blood was sizzling with desire and the two men had to be more than familiar with the feel of her body under their guiding hands. It was an amazing feeling.

"Let's take a short break before we begin the next one."

Gareth moved over to a small side table where a jug of wine and several earthen cups stood. He poured for each of them and served with good grace as Lars helped Belora to sit on the pretty, warm bricks that edged Kelvan's wallow. They had shown her about five different dances, each one progressively harder. They involved a bit more touching than she was used to, but touching two such handsome men was no hardship, she thought with an inward grin.

"Will I be expected to dance with other people?" she asked over the rim of her wine cup as Gareth sat down beside her.

"No. Just us. Lars is our third since he and Rohtina will be joining our family."

"I think Kelvan and Tina will enjoy the larger quarters. I went by there today and it's nicely situated." Lars sat beside them and gazed over the warm sands of the small wallow. "With two dragons sharing a home, they will require a much larger wallow and more room to move around."

"I'm going to start moving my stuff over tomorrow. How about you?" Gareth moved closer to her, pulling her back against his chest as his free arm tucked around her waist. She was surprised by the intimate move, but neither man seemed to think anything of it, so after a few moments, she relaxed back against him.

"I figured I'd do the same. Tina has some things she's collected over the years that she wants me to shift for her. Little sparkly stones and bits she's found in her journeys."

"Women of every species like their gems." Gareth and Lars chuckled, but Belora gasped as Gareth's large hand moved up to cup her breast. She couldn't believe he would fondle her in front of his friend, regardless of whether or not they were becoming some sort of family. She stiffened and would have pulled away, but Lars took her hand in his surprisingly gentle grasp and held her gaze.

"Don't be embarrassed. It is natural to be free amongst our family. I've accepted that I will never find a woman as Gareth has found you. Let me share in what you have together, at least in this way, for now."

"I'm not used to this. Your ways are very strange to me." She settled back against Gareth with a little trembling in her limbs, but didn't object further as his hand moved down inside the V of her blouse to cup her bare breast and flick the little bud so it stood out against the soft fabric. She knew Lars could see it clearly as his eyes dipped to focus on her nipples, blossoming under Gareth's skillful touch.

"I know, love, but this will be your home now. I hope you'll try to adjust to our ways." Gareth dipped to kiss her neck as he spoke softly next to her ear. "I won't rush you, but I need you to be open to new experiences. Can you do that for me? For us all?"

His hand squeezed her nipple hard and she felt little tremors of excitement course through her womb. She found she liked the hot flash of Lars' turquoise eyes as he licked his firm lips, his gaze glued to Gareth's manipulations under her shirt. It was definitely a new experience, but she found she wasn't afraid. She trusted Gareth with her very life. It was little stretch to trust him with her pleasure. He would never hurt her or make her do anything she didn't want to do. She knew that in her soul and it allowed her to let go and let him lead their pleasure.

She nodded as he moved his hand out of her blouse and turned her in his arms to face her. His eyes held hers and sought her answer.

"I trust you and I'll try."

A broad smile spread across his lips before they claimed hers in a deep, happy kiss. He lingered over her mouth before turning her once more in his arms. Lars had moved closer while they kissed and now he was only inches from her aroused body. Gareth pushed her gently toward his friend, encouraging her with his voice.

"Kiss Lars, sweet. Let him know there are no hard feelings. Welcome him to our family and let him know just a tiny bit of what we share."

She looked back at him questioningly, but his eyes were encouraging and his hands open, willing to let her decide whether she would go through with his suggestion or not. It was the freedom to choose that made her move forward. A kiss was a small thing, after all, and it was not like it was any kind of hardship to share a kiss with such a handsome and kind man. She turned back and smiled at Lars as she moved into his strong arms.

He clasped her against his chest and moved his head down, his turquoise eyes dazzling her as he drew closer, oh, so slowly. When his firm lips met hers, her eyes shut in self-defense as his scent, his feel, and his amazingly gentle touch flooded her senses with warmth. His lips caressed hers for a long moment before his tongue sought entrance, taking the kiss deeper. She was surprised but more than willing, swept up in the passion of the man and the moment.

Lars kissed like a dream. Gentle as only a very strong man can be, he tempered his strength with a deep passion that she could feel as his muscular arms trembled the tiniest bit. He made a small, inarticulate sound of pleasure as she wrapped her arms around him. It spurred her on and she answered the sweeping intimacies of his tongue in her mouth with her own daring forays into his warmth. She felt hot all over and realized vaguely that Gareth had moved up behind them, enclosing her between the two men. His hands teased her nipples and stoked her fire.

When at long last the kiss broke, all three were panting. Belora shot shocked eyes up to Lars and was greeted with a stunned smile.

"You are beautiful, milady, and much too good for a scoundrel like Gareth. I wish I had met you first."

She laughed and the tension of the moment was broken. She realized that while Gareth had been palming her breasts, Lars' hands were up under her skirts, skimming her legs. They now rested on her thighs, his fingers dangerously close to the juncture that wept with arousal.

"In the mating dance, you will be expected to kiss us both and we will both handle your body in ever more intimate ways—lifting you up in our arms, twirling you around, touching you all over. You must give over control to us completely." Gareth's breath pulsed against her ear and made her shiver. "Can you handle it?" He spoke it like a dare.

"I can handle it, but will everyone be watching?"

Lars nodded. "The mated pairs will be dancing with us, but the single knights will certainly enjoy the show, dreaming of the day they find their own mate and are able to claim her before the entire enclave. It's a rite of passage and something we do to solidify our families and share our pleasure with our fellows. It's important."

The earnestness of his words touched her heart. It made an odd sort of sense. His words made her want to perform this strange dance with these two strong men, for the good of the Lair.

"All right. I guess it won't be so bad if we're not the only ones doing it."

Gareth chuckled as he rose and lifted her up with him. Lars stood in front of her and they moved back to the cleared area where they'd been practicing before.

"We'll all be dressed differently of course, so we'll just pantomime some of the parts we can only do while in the ceremonial clothing."

Gareth moved in front of his mate-to-be and positioned her for the start of the dance. He was much closer to her than he had been for any of the other dances she'd learned that day, and Lars stood so close to her back, she could feel the warmth radiating from his body. She did the moves as they taught them to her but quickly realized just a few minutes into this strange dance that he was not kidding when he said she would have to give over control to them both.

After a few initial moves, she was simply swept off her feet by first Gareth, then Lars, passed between them as her feet barely touched the ground. The two brawny men did most of the work as they swung her around in their strong arms, her body held tight to their own while little tingles of electricity raced through her frame. Gareth made her burn with his slightest touch, but the look in Lars' blue eyes as he held her close nearly made her insides melt. The set of his jaw proclaimed how very hungry he was for her and she could feel his shocking erection against her abdomen.

"That's enough for now, I think." Gareth's voice was calm as he stood behind them. Lars' mesmerizing gaze was fused to her own. Gradually, he released her and she slid down his hard body to rest once more on unsteady feet. Her entire body trembled and she could feel that he was hard as granite against her. A muscle ticked in his jaw but otherwise he indicated none of his discomfort.

Gareth snuck his arm around her waist from behind and pulled her unresisting body back against him as she swayed on her feet. She was glad of his support, though her dazed eyes were still locked on Lars.

"We'll see you later, Lars. Thanks for your assistance." Gareth's words were formal but his tone was warm. She realized he knew exactly what afflicted his friend as he fit her bottom against his own raging hardness.

After a long moment Lars nodded, bowed slightly to her and left the chamber.

"Will he be all right?"

Gareth chuckled behind her, pulling her soft body closer against his. "Nothing a few strokes of his hand won't cure. Would you like to help him?"

She was shocked, but also titillated by the teasing remark. "Would you want me to?"

Gareth turned her in his arms. "Oh, yes. I'd enjoy watching that."

She stiffened in his arms. "You'd enjoy seeing me pleasure other men?"

"Not just any other man. Only Lars. He will be our family soon, Belora. It's only right that you should be able to share pleasure with him. It's normal and healthy for our kind."

"I don't understand your ways at all." She shook her head but relaxed once more against his hard body.

"It's all right. We have time yet." He hugged her close, tucking her head under his chin. "Does the idea repulse you, though? Could you make him welcome in our family, do you think?"

She snuggled into him. "He's so quiet, yet I sense in him a great well of feeling kept tightly under wraps. He's so alone." Her voice was quiet with thought and sympathy.

"Lars has been alone for a long time. His parents and siblings were killed right in front of him during the Northern Wars when he was only a small boy. His partner, Rohtina, found him among those left for dead a few days later. He was badly injured, but managed to cling to her back until she could get him back to the Lair. For years he spoke to no one but Rohtina, his dragon partner." Gareth sighed as he tucked her hair behind her ear and held her close. "He's only a year or so younger than me and we became friends early on when we were still just boys, really. Others thought him strange and it was hard for him to find welcome from some of the other knights, but we've been close friends for many years. I love him as a brother. I've never said the words to him, but I know he feels the same, though he rarely speaks at all."

"Now I begin to understand what lies beneath." Her mind spun and her heart opened with sympathy and a nurturing kind of love for Lars. It encompassed Gareth too, for the protective way he spoke of his heart-scarred friend.

"Because Rohtina will be Kelvan's mate, our friendship will now become a true partnership. We will be family, a fighting unit when on duty and a partnership in whatever we do. All five of us will live together in one large suite and any children we have will also be his to nurture and raise. When the dragonets come, likewise we will all help in whatever way Kel and Tina need us to. The five of us will be family in the truest sense."

"Am I expected to...uh...to have sex with him?" She didn't really know if she was nervous about the answer or excited. Either way, her breath was coming faster and something inside her tummy clenched in anticipation.

"Neither of us will ever force you to do anything you don't want to do."

"But is that how the other mated pairs work?"

"Most, yes. There are so few women among us that it's normal for one woman to be wife to both knights if their dragons are mated. Kel says the Mother of All knows what She's doing when She pairs off the dragons and their knights. But not all matings work the same way. There are no real rules about it. Each woman pretty much decides for herself what she's comfortable with and how the relationship will work. It'll be up to you, what you will allow. You could limit him to oral pleasure, or you could take him as you take me. Whatever you decide, when the dragons mate, you will have to adjust and find a way to help us both at the same time. The dragons' mating will affect us deeply and we will both need your help and understanding at those times. Ideally, it would be best if we could make love to you simultaneously, but again, that will be up to you."

His words and the deep tone of his voice made her squirm. She pressed her legs together and felt the wetness already on her thighs from this hot conversation. She realized it wasn't fear that made her feel this way. No, she rather liked the idea of what Gareth was proposing. She'd felt the same instant attraction to Lars as she had felt the moment she had seen Gareth. Something about both men called out to her—heart and soul. It was not logical, but it *was*, nonetheless. Something about them felt right and good. She would be a fool not to explore where this might lead.

"Do you really want this? Wouldn't you be jealous if I took him as my lover?"

Gareth stared down at her with serious eyes. "If you took any other man as a lover, I would kill him outright." She gasped at the deadly intent in his eyes. "But Lars is my brother now. Our dragon partners are going to be mates. It's inevitable that the three of us will be caught up in the fever as our dragon partners mate, and they'll do so often once they're finally free to join. I couldn't let Lars face that alone. I must admit the idea of watching you with him, of filling you at the same time as he does, excites me. There's no other man I would share you with. Only him. I know that if I should fall in battle, he'll be there to take care of you and vice versa. We're a team now. The Mother of All has ordained it. We'll both love you until the day we die, if you let us."

Belora thought about Gareth's shocking words as they ate and later as he led her to the communal hot baths. She had heard about them, of course, but had not visited the hot springs yet herself.

The cavern was larger than she'd expected, and the main

pool was absolutely huge. It could have qualified as a small lake, she thought, but the bubbling, effervescent surface and slightly metallic tang of the humid air made it much different from any other lake she had ever seen.

There were a few men already in the water, and they all looked up as Gareth and Belora entered. Several shouted greetings to Gareth or lifted their hands to wave while eyeing Belora with great interest. She began to wonder just how this bathing business was supposed to be accomplished without great embarrassment. She tugged on Gareth's hand and he stopped to look down at her.

"I hope you don't expect me to get naked in front of all of them." Her whispered words carried to him alone, though she knew all the men present watched them closely.

"There's no shame in nakedness, Belora. Besides, remember what I said before? I think I'll enjoy knowing that my friends and comrades can look but never touch my mate. Many of them may never find mates of their own. Seeing the happiness of others is the only real glimpse of joy left to them besides the momentary pleasure they can find with a whore or some other random woman who doesn't mind the great huge dragon lurking about outside in her garden, scaring the neighbors."

Belora giggled at the picture he painted with his words and his lips softened into a loving smile. He stroked back her hair and caressed her cheek.

"Besides, we won't be in the main pool. There are smaller pools designed for a bit more privacy. We'll use one of those."

"Will they be able to see us?"

"Maybe. If they are in the right spot."

She chuckled. "How much do you want to bet they'll all want to move suddenly to the one area from which they can see me naked?"

"You've got a point there." He chuckled as she did. "But then, you'll be seeing them naked too, so it kind of evens out."

"Hmm." She looked around his broad body to get another exaggerated look at the muscular men sitting or wading in the fairly shallow water near the edge. "I hadn't thought of that. That blonde man has a spectacular ass. Do you think he'll mind me ogling him?"

"He might not, but I certainly will." Gareth growled with a grin as he chased her toward the far end of the cavern where the more private pools lay.

A bit breathless from both the exertion and the heat of the cavern, she came to a sudden halt before one of the pools. Lars was there. Already naked and in the water.

"And when were you going to tell me about this?" She arched her brow and looked from Lars to Gareth with teasing accusation in her eyes. She gasped aloud when Lars stood from the water, his nude body gleaming wetly in the low light of the cavern. He was solid muscle and had a long, thick cock. He was already rock hard.

"I'll leave if you wish it."

He made to step out of the pool but halted when Belora took one almost unconscious step toward him, her gaze focused on his cock. She realized this was another part of Gareth's plan to make her aware of the things that would be expected of her as his wife and get her used to Lars as well. As far as plans went, she had to agree it was a good one. A woman would have to be dead not to be attracted to the masculine perfection and puppy-like eagerness of them both. They wanted so much to please her and for her to accept them. It was touching really. And very flattering.

"Don't leave, Lars. If I'm really going to marry into this world, I need to know if I can handle it, right?" She turned around and punched Gareth in the arm. "Don't think I don't recognize your plotting hand in this little scene, but in this case, I'll forgive you. I'm willing to try and see where this goes. He can stay, but if I want to call a halt at any time, you have to promise to stop."

"Of course." Gareth pulled her close and hugged her. "Your wishes will always come first. Always."

She nodded against his chest and stroked his arms. "I thought you'd say that, but I had to be sure. This is kind of scary for me."

He soothed her and hugged her tightly. "You're so brave, my sweet." He bent to whisper in her ear. "I love you so much. Do you realize how very special you are to me? I will never love again. Only you, Belora. For the rest of our lives."

He kissed her then, pouring all his love into his kiss and she clung to him. Before she knew it, she felt the wafting warm air of the cave against her bare skin. Gareth had tugged her robe away until she was standing naked in his strong arms. Her gaze shot to Lars as Gareth pulled back, easing from their kiss.

Lars watched her every move, his eyes dark turquoise in the dim light, his gaze intense as he saw her nude body for the first time. Gareth spun her in his arms and pulled her back against his front, wrapping one muscular forearm around her waist as the other hand moved up to cup her breast, displaying her for his friend.

Entranced by the look on Lars' angular face, Belora felt a slick wetness seeping down the insides of her thighs. She had never been so excited by the mere look of a man before. Lars eased back into the water, seating himself on an underwater ledge at the far side of the small pool, one hand disappearing under the transparent surface to curve around his hard cock, stroking slowly as he watched Belora in Gareth's arms.

She licked her lips, thinking of forbidden things. But perhaps they weren't so forbidden after all. If she was going to go through with this, she could have both of these handsome, heart-strong men all to herself for the rest of their lives. Something deep down felt warm and secure at the thought, yet her mind worried over how such a relationship would work.

"Don't think so hard, sweet." Gareth's warm breath puffed against her ear as he spoke and his hands caressed her, the one at her waist slipping down to tease the neat curls at the juncture of her thighs. "Just feel."

He slipped his fingers into her folds, and her knees went weak. One hand squeezed one nipple, the other tugged on her clit, and her eyes closed in yearning ecstasy. Slowly, he moved his fingers over her, pressing and rotating in little swirls over the sensitive flesh, making her squirm. The hand on her breast dropped downward and then he was spreading her pussy wide, allowing Lars to see everything he was doing between her legs, showcasing her responsive clit for the other man.

"See how he looks at you? If you let him, he would lick your clit while I sucked on your nipples."

The words inflamed her and she groaned, shivering in his arms. Her eyes opened to see Lars stroking himself under the water more firmly now, his gaze feasting on the sight of her feminine core as Gareth used two fingers to probe deep inside her. She was slick with excitement and his passage was made easier by the fact that she was near peak from nothing more than his stroking and Lars' hot gaze.

He pumped his fingers into her tight core a few more times before she came on his hand, stifling her cry against his shoulder as he supported her spasming body. He held her, crooning to her as he pulled his fingers from her body, bringing them to his lips and licking them.

"Mmm. Delicious." He turned her slightly in his arms and brought the still wet fingers to her mouth. "Taste," he whispered. "Suck them clean." She opened her lips as his fingers pushed inside. She tasted herself on his flesh and the look in his eyes nearly drove her wild.

"Do you have any idea what you do to me?"

He removed his fingers and kissed her deeply. A moment later, her world spun as he hoisted her up in his arms and stepped into the pool. He lowered her into the warm water, supporting her as she learned the feel of the warm mineral springs. She smiled at him, still a bit nervous of the other man sharing the private pool, watching them from the other end. There were a few feet between where Gareth held her and Lars sat watching. It would be so easy to bridge that space physically, but mentally she just wasn't quite ready.

"The water's so warm and bubbly." She marveled at the feel of tiny bubbles bursting against her skin, leaving her feeling clean and relaxed.

"It's fed from the earth below with just a bit of magic to keep it warm and flowing."

"It's wonderful," she replied, meaning it. Everything about the Lair enchanted her.

"Not nearly as wonderful as you, Belora." Gareth's impassioned words touched her heart.

She smiled as he levered himself away and sat on the ledge of the pool, his hard cock standing upright for her to admire. She licked her lips again, wanting nothing more than to taste him as she had once before. Her eyes must have spoken of her desire because he chuckled and pulled her between his spread knees, his legs wrapping around her and crossing at the ankles behind her back.

"Oh, yes, I can see we both want the same thing. Taste me, Belora. Take me in your sweet mouth."

He guided her head gently toward his cock and she liked the way her breasts felt caressed by the millions of tiny bubbles in the water. She tingled all over as his hands tangled in her hair, urging her to do what she wanted. With a sigh of satisfaction, she placed her lips around his hard cock, sliding down and using her tongue the way he had coached her to do. Satisfaction filled her when he groaned in pleasure.

She knew Lars could see every movement. The thought didn't disturb her as much as she thought it would. In fact, it tickled her sense of adventure and made her want to give him a show worth remembering. The idea that he was so close, so much a part of this even though he was only an observer, made her hot.

No doubt about it. She was wanton.

She smiled around Gareth's cock as she realized it was he who had awakened these raging desires within her. Gareth was her first lover, but if he had his way, she would take Lars before long, as well. At first the thought had shocked and scared her, but now that she was getting to know the strong, silent knight, the idea was more and more appealing. She wondered what his cock would taste like and how he would respond to her sucking. Maybe, she thought with a blush and a feeling of inevitability, it was time to find out.

Gareth stopped her with a slight tug on her hair. A surprising disappointment swept through her, but she trusted him to lead their love play. He knew things about lovemaking that she had never experienced and she would follow his lead.

"As much as I enjoy the feel of your mouth on me, if we don't stop now, I'll come much sooner than I'd like."

He dropped back into the pool and brought his lips to hers, working her around in the water until they were just a few feet from Lars. Gareth's strong arms lifted her out of the water and set her on the edge of the pool. She was surprised by the sudden move and grabbed onto his shoulders for balance, but his smile set her at ease and reignited the fires in her belly. Sweet Mother, how she loved this man!

"Are you ready for me, sweet?" Holding her gaze, he parted

her pussy lips with one hand and entered her channel with the fingers of the other. He smiled devilishly as her slick wetness coated his fingers. "You want my cock, Belora? Tell me if you do."

"Yes," she whimpered.

"Yes? What do you want, love? Tell me." His eyes challenged her, while his fingers continued to tease.

"I want your cock, Gareth. In me. I want it now." Her whispered words seemed to galvanize him.

He stepped up onto the ledge that put him at the perfect height to slide home into her with one solid thrust. She cried out as he slid home, only then realizing that Lars was standing right beside them, watching all in intimate detail as his hand squeezed his rampant cock.

Her eyes locked with Lars' turquoise gaze for a long moment and she realized that his presence seemed somehow right. Only one thing could make it better—if he could find satisfaction at the same time they did.

"Let me," she whispered, bringing both knights' eyes to her face. Gareth followed the direction of her gaze and nodded at Lars, a broad smile spreading across his strong lips.

Lars wasted no time, moving to stand at the edge of the pool, his hard length level with her mouth. She knew he was giving her the choice of how she would pleasure him and her slight uncertainty made her want to start slow. She brought one hand up to circle his pulsing cock as Gareth resumed stroking in and out of her pussy. His hands and mouth teased her nipples while Lars watched, the only contact between them her hand on his cock.

She realized Lars was letting her call the shots, allowing her to decide how far this would go. The thought made her feel safe and cherished. And powerful. This strong man was allowing her to choose what she would give him, with no complaint. The idea humbled and warmed her, showing her without words how noble a man he really was.

Leaning slightly, she licked his length and looked up into his smoldering eyes. Holding his gaze, she took him deep in her mouth and used her tongue to learn his shape, his taste, and his feel. He was spectacular.

She sucked him deep as Gareth thrust into her core, bringing her closer and closer to orgasm. She knew when she flew to the stars this time, she would take both of these special, beloved men with her. Gareth sucked one nipple and pinched the other hard as he drove into her faster and faster. She felt her climax starting from deep within and she pulled hard on Lars' hot cock, coaxing his climax with the suction of her mouth. He came as she did, followed only seconds later by Gareth's spurting deep inside her womb.

The three of them lounged in the pool for long moments, enjoying the restorative power of the bubbly water. They sat on the ledge, each slightly submerged, Gareth's arm thrown casually around Belora's shoulder as his hand dipped down to toy with her nipple. Lars sat on her other side, not touching, but watching her with a renewed heat and pure male appreciation.

"Thank you." Lars' soft voice came to her from out of the dimness of the cavern, making her look over to meet his intense gaze.

She smiled softly at him and leaned up to kiss his lips sweetly. He took the kiss deeper, and she slipped into his arms for a long, languid moment.

"I don't know yet if I can go much further with this, Lars." She pulled away from him to sit on her own between the two men. She had to tell them what was going on in her mind. She didn't want them getting the wrong idea that suddenly she was okay with the crazy lifestyle in the Lair. "I'll be brutally honest with you. Now that things have cooled a bit, I'm a little shocked by what I just did, but it felt good. I don't regret it, but I have to think about this a bit more."

Gareth's hand stroked her wet hair. "Take the time you need, my love. I'm sorry if you feel pressured. We don't mean to rush you."

"I don't feel pressured, but it's a lot to take in all at once. Just give me some more time, okay? I didn't want you assuming I was fine with everything when in my mind I still have some reservations."

Lars smiled kindly at her. "Honesty in all things is important between mates."

Feeling somewhat better, she dipped into the pool, bathing her hair in the effervescent water. After a few more relaxing minutes, they all gathered their robes and left the pool. Gareth and Belora headed for his suite and Lars walked away toward where his dragon waited.

Chapter Six

When Gareth and Kelvan took off for patrol early the next morning, Belora went to visit her mother in Kelzy's suite.

"I heard you went to the springs last eve." Kelzy's voice sounded in the minds of both mother and daughter, though Adora knew the dragon was speaking of her daughter's activities. The blush staining Belora's fair cheeks amused her, but she also felt a pang of regret for her little girl who was now a woman grown.

"Um...yes. It was very educational."

Kelzy snorted smoke in dragonish laughter. *"I bet."*

"Mama Kelzy, are you teasing my girl?" Adora gathered her daughter close for a long hug. "I've missed you, honey girl. What have you been doing with yourself?"

"Trying to decide if I'm going to stay."

Belora looked so torn. Adora kept her arm around her shoulders and guided her to sit with her at the edge of Kelzy's wallow. She shot a concerned glance to the dragon.

"I thought your mating feast was set for this evening."

"It is, but I'm just not sure I can go through with it." Her eyes looked pained and confused.

"Why not?"

"Oh, Mama, it's so different here. The things they expect of me... I just don't know if it's right or if I can do it."

"What things?" Adora's voice held all the anger of an enraged mother hen. She had spent most of her life protecting this girl. She'd done the best she could to raise her strong and comfortable in herself. She couldn't fathom what the knights or dragons would ask of her that would put such fear and self-doubt in her eyes, but she didn't like it. Indignation filled her, the inner fire that she usually kept well banked, rising to take on anyone who would hurt her baby.

Belora blushed a fiery red. "Um...sexual things. There are so few women here, you see. And when Kelvan mates, they expect me to...oh, this is hard to talk about, even with you, Mama."

Kelzy shook her head and sighed warm air around them. Adora pinned her with a steely gaze.

"Just what is making my brave baby girl so confused? And what has your son to do with it?"

Kelzy shifted in her wallow. *"It's always hardest on those not raised in a Lair. Adora, you have to realize the bond between dragon and knight is soul deep. What he feels, we feel and vice versa. When Jared takes a woman, I feel it and if I'm ever lucky enough to be able to mate again, it will undoubtedly drive Jared into an uncontrollable lust. That's why fighting dragons—those of us partnered with knights—are forbidden to mate unless our knights have a wife. When the lust rides us all, the knights will turn to their wife to share the mating fever safely."*

"Wife? Only one wife for two knights?"

Kelzy nodded her great head. *"There are so few women who can live among dragons. Our knights have learned to share. But their love and protection for their wife runs deeper than any regular tie. They live dangerous lives. If one knight falls, he knows his partner will be there to take care of their wife and children. It's the way of fighting knights and dragons. It has been this way for centuries."*

"Well, that's some dirty little secret you have there." Adora was shocked, but turned over the problem in her mind. "So just who else is my baby expected to marry tonight?"

"His name is Lars." Belora's voice was reserved, her face flushed and eyes confused. "He's wonderful, Mama. Really. He's quiet and so thoughtful and he has the gentlest heart."

"You sound half in love with him already!" Adora was scandalized and more than a little intrigued. Still, it didn't sit quite right, her inexperienced baby girl being expected to welcome two brawny knights into her life and her bed.

Belora seemed to think about it. "You know, maybe I am. Gareth brought him around and helped us get to know each other. I like him a lot, but I don't know if I can let them both..." She trailed off in embarrassment once more.

"They are expected to have her at the same time?" Adora turned accusing eyes to the dragon.

"When the mating heat is upon them all, it will be inevitable. Most of the human women involved in such arrangements seem to enjoy it immensely. Think of the benefits, child. Two men at your beck and call at all times. Two men who will love you and put your happiness and safety above their own. Two men to help around the Lair and father your babies."

"This isn't some kind of perverted partner-swapping thing, is it?" Adora wanted to know.

"By the Mother, where do you get such notions? Of course it isn't! Once mated, knights remain true to their mates for the rest of their lives. This isn't some whim. The Mother guides the knights in their selection of a mate, just as She guides us dragons. Is it any wonder your daughter already has feelings for the knight of my son's future mate? The Mother of All knows what She is doing, after all."

"I love Gareth, Mama. I loved him almost from the first moment I saw him and I want to spend the rest of my life with him. But I feel things for Lars too. It's hard to describe. He's so different from Gareth, so special. I want to bring him out of his shell and tease him until he laughs. He doesn't laugh nearly enough. I like his kisses and I love the way he treats me as if I'm made of spun glass."

Adora didn't know what to think, but the look in her daughter's eyes was oddly reassuring. "I think I need to meet this Lars."

"He'll be here in a few minutes. I just asked Rohtina, his partner, to bring him here. She wants to meet Belora too, by the way. How could a sensible man like Gareth overlook introducing the two females who will be expected to share a suite? I thought he was smarter than that. Honestly!"

Kelzy huffed while the two human women listened to the sounds of an approaching dragon. Apparently, Rohtina was prompt and somewhat eager to meet them if her fast tread was any indication. When she came through the huge archway, Adora caught her breath.

She was a gorgeous young dragon in a golden red hue that shone like the morning sun. Her eyes were amber jewels, bright with intelligence and eagerly taking in all there was to see. Intelligence sparkled there and a perky humor, if she didn't miss her guess.

Adora and her daughter stood to greet Rohtina with a formal bow, which was graciously returned. Straightening, Adora noted the tall blonde man at the dragon's side. No wonder her daughter was half in love with him already. He was even more beautiful than his dragon partner. These two together shone like the sun. Between her iridescent golden red scales and his silvery blonde perfection, they were nearly blinding.

Adora strode forward. "Lady Rohtina, I've just learned that your knight expects to be mated to my daughter."

"This is true, Madam." The dragon projected her thoughts to all in the room. Her voice was melodic and gentle, quite different from Kelzy's more martial tone.

"You'll understand that I raised my daughter with quite a different expectation than having two husbands?"

"That is my understanding, but you must also understand that things are different among knights and dragons."

"Don't you dare to lecture my girl, Tina," Kelzy interjected with a hint of amusement. "Though she doesn't understand Lair life, she knows more about our kind than most of the knights."

Rohtina bowed her head in respect to the older dragon. *"If you say so."*

At this point, Belora broke out laughing. Lars chuckled too, followed by the rest of them. Belora moved forward to face the pretty female dragon.

"I like you, Lady Rohtina. You've got spirit."

"I like the way you make my knight feel. I don't think he's ever been this happy or hopeful."

Lars' fair skin flushed at his dragon partner's candid words, but Belora moved forward to take his hand in hers. She brought him to her mother and made introductions, including him in the group of females. Adora saw immediately that this young man had hidden depths. From the way his shoulders relaxed, Belora's touch obviously comforted him. She also liked the gentle way he cradled her daughter's small hand in his own.

"What are your intentions toward my daughter?" Adora asked boldly.

"Mother!"

"No, Belora, she has every right to ask such a question." Lars raised Belora's hand, stroking her palm soothingly. "My intention is to love her and protect her all of our lives. I will be true to her, cherish her, and put her happiness above my own."

"But you've only just met." Adora didn't understand how her sensible baby girl could fall in love with two men in nearly as many days, much less how those two men could claim to love her just as deeply, just as fast.

"Gareth knew her the moment he saw her. It's the way of knights to know their mate almost on sight. I like to think I would have recognized her too, had I been the first to meet her. As it stands, since Rohtina told me of her intention to mate with Kelvan, I've been introduced and found time to get to know Belora. But my heart knew her already. When I first looked into her eyes, I knew I'd found what I'd been seeking all my life."

"Why didn't you say anything before now?" Belora's whisper carried in the quiet room.

Lars shrugged, his turquoise eyes locking on her as if she were the only one in the room. "It wasn't yet time. Now it is. You're ready to hear it and I'm ready to say it. I love you, Belora. If you let me, I'll love you truly for the rest of our lives." He sank down to one knee, humbling himself before her. "Will you be my wife?"

Tears streamed down her face as Belora reached down and kissed Lars on the lips, dragging him upward so she could put her arms around his thick, muscular frame. He wrapped her in his arms and kissed her deeply, holding her close as the others watched, knowing they had been forgotten.

"Just for the record, you understand, what's your answer?" Kelzy's amused voice broke them apart.

"Oh, I think she said yes, Mama Kelzy." Adora leaned comfortably against Kelzy's sparkling foreleg, watching her daughter with amusement.

Lars and his partner seemed to be surprised by Adora's familiarity with the older dragon.

"Well, I think that's settled, isn't it?" Kelzy added, satisfaction in her rumbling tone.

"I'm still not totally sure I'm comfortable with this two husband arrangement."

"Child, do you trust me?" Kelzy asked Adora point blank.

"Well, of course I trust you. You raised me, didn't you?" Again the two newcomers were surprised by the conversation, but didn't interrupt.

"Then trust me on this. It's the way of Lair life and no hardship on the woman, I can assure you. Your daughter will come to no harm with her two mates and will, in all likelihood, be very happy."

"You promise?" Adora held out her little human hand to the huge dragon.

"I promise." Kelzy put one huge talon carefully into the woman's hand and they shook once as if in some childhood ritual. It was totally charming and utterly strange behavior for a fighting dragon—especially one of Kelzy's stature.

"Well, all right then." Adora swiped at a stray tear that had leaked from the corner of her eye.

"Now off with you three. Adora and I have plans to discuss for tonight and plots to hatch." Kelzy swept one of her great wings toward the entrance, shooing her guests out.

Belora hugged her mother once and headed out with Lars and his dragon partner.

"Your mother is definitely an interesting woman," he mused as he settled his arm around her waist.

"Lady Kelzy practically raised her from the time she was just a toddler 'til she was about ten years old."

"Kelzy? Raise a human child? The others talk about her strange ways but I didn't realize there was some truth to the tales."

"Lady Kelzy was the best thing that ever happened to my mother." Belora defended her mother and the older dragon fiercely. "She has a kind heart and a pure soul. If the other dragons have a problem with that then they're just bigoted idiots."

Rohtina stopped short on the wide ledge they were traversing to turn her large head toward Belora. She blinked her golden amber eyes down at her for a moment, considering her.

"You're brave for a human female. I think we'll get along just fine."

Rohtina moved to the edge of the cliff and launched herself magnificently into the sky while Lars and Belora watched.

"Either she hates me or we're starting to find some common ground," Belora observed.

Lars reached down and placed a kiss on her hair. "Oh, she likes you all right. You just passed her test."

"That was a test?" She spun in Lars' arms to look up at him as he nodded.

"She holds Kelzy in high esteem. You probably don't realize it, but Kelzy and her partner Jared are the leaders of this Lair. They oversaw its construction and Kelzy leads the dragons here. She holds a lot of power and is one of the most respected dragons in the land. She serves the royal family directly. Others may gossip about her sometimes undragonish ways, but my Tina admires her greatly. She wants to be just like her, and of course Kelvan is a lot like his mama, and she loves Kelvan."

"I had no idea."

"Tina's hard to read until you get to know her."

"Sort of like her partner, you mean?" Belora teased him with her smile.

He nodded with a self-conscious grin. "I'd have to admit you're probably right on that one."

It warmed her heart to see his smile. She reached up and palmed his cheek, urging him down so she could place a light kiss on his lips. One kiss turned to two, then two turned to more until they were all but necking right in the open, for anyone to see.

Gareth came upon them long moments later, his chuckle finally penetrating the fog of desire that swirled around them.

"I see you two have come to terms."

Belora eased down and a little apart from Lars. Both were breathing hard.

"I asked her to be my wife and she agreed," Lars reported, never removing his hot gaze from her.

Gareth slapped his friend on the back in congratulations, but Lars was so solidly built it barely made an impression. Gareth grinned happily when Belora finally tore her gaze from Lars to realize they'd drawn a small crowd of onlookers.

Single knights were watching them, some with appreciation, some with longing in their eyes. It was disconcerting at first until she realized all looked on them with true happiness that their fellows had found a woman to share their lives. She realized in that moment that she, in a small way, represented hope for them all. Hope that they would find women willing to be their wives and share their lives.

No doubt it was hard for most human women to accept dragons in their midst, but the idea of having two husbands was also a bit daunting. Daunting and exciting at the same time.

The mating feast was a grand affair. Every soul in the Lair had gathered in the communal area, up on the bluff above the main entrance to the Lair. Up on the flat, there was enough room for all the dragons and the humans as well. A huge fire had been lit at the center of the gathering along with several smaller ones for cooking and for those who wished more intimate circles, but the guests of honor were in the center, where the dancing was.

Belora and her new mates had already danced all of the dances they'd taught her during her brief lesson, some three and four times. The party in full swing, the other mated trios joined them while the unmated knights watched and clapped their hands in time with the music. Belora felt the pull of the men's eyes on her, but her full attention focused on her two mates and on the two mighty dragons who watched, their necks twining together as their own passions rose steadily through the evening.

There had been excellent food served to them as the celebration began, joined by fine wines and beers, and even sweets for dessert. Then the tables had been cleared away to make room for the raucous dancing. But first, the ceremony.

As the elders of the Lair, Kelzy and Jared waited in the center of the clearing, the huge dragon a witness and support behind her knight, the General of the winged forces of this Lair. It was before Jared they would promise themselves to each other and with his words of blessing, they would officially be wed.

The ceremonial words were short, but no less beautiful for their brevity. Belora's mother wept openly as she watched her little girl pledge her life to the two magnificent knights that stood tall and strong at her sides. Gareth and Lars took turns promising their love and protection for all time to the woman they both loved and then it was the dragons' turn.

Kelvan and his beautiful Rohtina stood behind the humans, surrounding them and protecting them as they shared in the joining ceremony. They pledged their lives to each other in the presence of Kelzy and Jared, receiving slightly altered words of blessing from the dragon in return for their promises to share their fire and their flight with only each other for as long as their knights and their mate should live.

Belora realized belatedly that dragon joining had to depend

101

greatly on the humans involved—at least among fighting dragons who were paired with human knights. Since dragons lived far longer than their human partners, they could mate only while the humans had their own partners, unless they wanted to break the laws that bound human and dragon together and drive their bonded partner insane with need at the same time. It was just not done. Belora shed a tear when she realized just how greatly the dragons sacrificed to protect their human partners and what such a partnership really meant.

"Whom the Mother has joined, in Her wisdom, let none put asunder." Jared's voice boomed out so that all could hear, echoed by Kelzy's triumphant trumpeting call. The other dragons joined in, howling their happiness to the heavens as the ceremony concluded and Belora felt the thunder of their call rumble through her body. It was an amazing feeling.

Moments later, the dancing began in earnest and her new mates swept her up into their strong arms and twirled her around and around, making her dizzy with happiness. She danced with them and noticed the other trios joining them in the space set aside for dancing. There were more family groups in the Lair than she had realized. Every woman she had met was on the dance floor with two knights each and she realized that there were no single women in the Lair, only a wealth of single men who had little hope of finding a mate who could fit in with their odd lifestyle.

They had been dancing for hours, though it was such fun it seemed like only a few minutes to Belora. Her two men had grown increasingly bold as the night wore on, handling her body with possession and a masterful strength that excited her blood more than she had thought possible. Lars was coming out of his shell more and more too, it seemed, equal with Gareth on every count both in his provocative actions and in her heart.

Before the feast, they had gifted her with a special outfit, crafted of the finest, softest leather. It was a strange garment, consisting of a short, floaty skirt and a halter top covered by a wrap that preserved her modesty on top. She had been afraid she might be cold, but the fires and increased tempo of the dancing kept her warm as the night wore on.

When the mating dance began, she did the few steps required of her, then gave herself almost completely over to the control of her two men. Smiling up into their faces as they lifted and twirled her around, passing her from one to the other of them, she was warmed by the love and fire flashing back from their eyes to hers.

At one point, they let her back on her feet for a moment. Gareth twirled her about, stealing the wrap from about her upper body, leaving her clad only in the brief halter and skirt. She gasped as the night wind caressed her body, but only a moment later she was twirled into Lars' strong arms. He held her close against his warm chest. His shirt had disappeared and her skin brushed his with longing. When she next saw Gareth, his shirt was gone as well.

The dance progressed, their flesh making contact in tantalizing, mesmerizing, and gratifying brushes that only heightened her excitement and desire for her men. She wanted them. Oh, how she wanted them! Separately, together, however she could get them.

"Now we come to it, my love." Gareth spoke in a low, harsh voice as he held her off her feet, her breasts soft against his hard, bare chest. "The dance is nearly over and the true wedding rite begins."

Lars pressed up behind her, sandwiching her body between them. Her eyes widened and all around them she noted that the other married trios were in the same position. The dance ended, but all held quiet while the dragons around them began their trumpeting calls. Two by two, the dragons were twining their necks around each other, moving off toward the ledge from which they could easily launch skyward. Two by two, they took to the sky, their knight partners and their mate disappearing from the dance floor to seek the shadowed bowers that were a natural part of the bluff.

Last to seek the sky were the newly mated Kelvan and Rohtina. When they beat their great wings in time and launched skyward, all the unmated dragons bellowed and breathed fire up to the stars in a magnificent send-off. As Kel and Tina took to the air, Belora was lifted in her mates' arms and led to the beautiful bower in the shelter of magnificent fir trees that had been reserved for them alone this night of nights.

The married women of the Lair had prepared this special love nest with all the comforts of their home below, decorating it specially for this one perfect night. Soft pillows covered a bed of piled furs. Lars lifted her high and placed her gently on the center of the fur bed, coming down almost immediately to one side while Gareth claimed the other. Both men had fire in their eyes as their dragons twined around each other in an intricate dance in the sky.

Belora knew that both knights were intimately bound to their dragons and that as the dragons' lust grew, so would theirs. The other women had warned her that this first time could be somewhat overwhelming since both dragons were very young and had never mated before. The dragons might not realize how their passions would inflame their partners or themselves and they could easily work themselves and their knights into a frenzy before morning.

The women said this uniformly with a twinkle in their eye and a look almost of longing, while reassuring Belora that she would enjoy every single moment of it. But the caution remained. They warned her not to deny the knights this one, most important night of their union. This night, she must remain passive and allow the men their ease. All the women assured her that taking a passive role, at least this once, would be more rewarding than she could imagine and she trusted their judgment. After all, these women had lived through it. They knew what they were talking about. She would have to trust their judgment in this and in other things as she learned from them the everyday ways of life in the Lair.

Gareth turned her in his arms and kissed her deeply. She moaned and writhed as Lars' hands began a slow torture of the flesh of her hips and lower. One of his hands slipped between the cheeks of her ass, teasing the puckered hole there, while the other played in her pussy, slipping and sliding in her eager readiness.

"Tell me you want this," Gareth breathed when he let her up for air, his eyes blazing with fire into her own. "Tell me you want us both."

"I do!" Her voice was a squeak of pleasure as Lars dipped his fingers deep inside her pussy, pulsing and scissoring through her sensitive tissues. "I want you both."

Gareth sat back, glancing over at Lars as some kind of unspoken communication seemed to pass between the two. Lars pulled back as well and she could see the fire reflected in his turquoise eyes, now burning with golden flickers as he watched her.

"We talked about this." Gareth caressed her face as if he could not help but touch her in some way. "Lars gets your pussy first, I'll come behind. He wants to be inside you so badly, Belora. As do I."

"Behind?" She squealed just a bit as Lars' incredibly strong hands grasped her roughly and turned her toward him. He didn't hurt her. He couldn't hurt her. He was so gentle, even with all his vast strength. But she thrilled at the small hint of roughness, the only clue he gave her that he was near the edge of his control. She liked the idea more than she could say.

"Yes, Belora." Gareth stroked her ass cheeks as Lars pulled her on top of him, adjusting her legs so she straddled his massive body. His thick erection nestled just at the apex of her thighs, waiting impatiently to go where it longed to bury itself inside her. Gareth's hands, meanwhile, stroked between her cheeks, slathering a warm, slippery substance that smelled faintly of cinnamon, making his path easier as he probed into her. She gasped. It felt surprisingly good.

"I'm going to take your ass this time," he went on to say, all the while playing inside her, bringing her passions to a new level, "while Lars has your pussy. It's something I've wanted for a long time. I've dreamed of this moment, my love. Of making you come around us both so hard, you forget your own name. Forget anything existed beyond the pleasure we could give you."

She must have seemed frightened, for Lars tightened his strong arms around her, bringing her eyes to his. He kissed her softly, his fire receding for the tiniest moment while he seemed to assure himself that she was truly okay.

"If you don't want this, just say the word." Lars kissed her softly, coaxing her to tell him the truth of her feelings. "We'll never hurt you, my love. We want only your pleasure."

She kissed him back with more pressure, hoping to bring that fire back to his eyes. Squirming, she was able to take just the tip of his bulging cock inside her pussy as she did her best to inflame him. She lifted her head to view her handiwork, smiling down at him.

"I trust you both. More than that, I love you. I know you won't hurt me." She pecked at the corner of his lips, biting lightly, glad to see the fire leap once more, even brighter in his eyes. "If you two want this and think it will increase my pleasure, I believe you." She leaned just a little father back—as far as Lars' tight arms would let her go and turned her head to wink up at Gareth who appeared to be listening closely. "Do your worst, boys."

She giggled as Lars clamped down with his arms, bringing her body tight against his as he kissed her long and deep.

Gareth went back to preparing her back entrance and she was able to take just a bit more of Lars' hot hardness within her aching sheath.

How she wanted them!

She heard a far off roar and knew the dragons were nearing their own peaks of ecstasy. Lars grunted and slid all the way inside her. She was surprised at the sudden move, but thrilled by the feel of him, so wide and thick inside her. He felt different from Gareth, but just as sexy and exciting. How she loved them both!

"You fit around him like a glove, Belora." Gareth's words were harsh behind her. "Now take me too. Relax, open and take me, my love."

He pushed gently, but with firm pressure against the small opening he had made wider with his gliding touch. It was hard at first for her to accept this, but she knew she must. The other wives had warned her in not so many words about this sort of thing, each admitting that great pleasure could be had from letting the men have their way. Keeping that in mind, along with her ever-expanding love for both of these warriors, she relaxed and submitted to their pleasure in whatever way they would take it.

Gareth eased inside, a harsh groan coming from his lips as he seated himself fully within Belora's tight, virgin ass.

"Yes, that's it. Sweet Mother, Belora!"

Both men began to move as the fire from their dragons intensified. Bonded on a soul-deep level with the great beasts that even now tangled in the air high above, mating in a frenzy that could kill them if they didn't finish in time to break apart and spread their wings to fly high once more. The free fall of dragon mating was something he had never experienced before, though the older knights talked about it once in a while. Feeling the echoes of Kelvan's pleasure through their link, and the incredible pleasure he was finding within Belora's willing body, was amazing.

No words could do this sensation justice. For a moment, he felt completely joined. As he was joined to Kel, so was Kel joined to Tina and Tina to Lars. Through the thin links that joined them, he could almost feel echoes of what Lars was feeling, and he knew exactly when to press down and when to retreat to bring them all the most pleasure.

His eyes sought Lars' and an understanding passed between them. They were already as close as brothers, but this experience bonded them anew. He could feel the other man through the thin barrier of Belora's body that separated them and he knew Lars' heart and the love that mirrored his own for the small woman giving them so much of her trust, heart and love. In that moment he knew this partnership was right. They were a family now and would be together until they died.

The dragons came in a rush of pleasure that seemed to go on and on and it fired the passions in both Gareth and Lars. He felt all four of them explode in his mind even as he felt Belora reaching out to join them. Her mind opened and then suddenly, she was part of the tenuous link they all shared, part of the family of dragons and knights.

Gareth was astounded as the pleasure they all felt doubled back and mirrored itself through each one of them. It was like nothing he'd ever heard described. It was completely unique. It was devastating.

He came with a harsh groan as Lars continued to pump his release into their wife's wondrous body. She shuddered around both of them, coaxing them yet higher even as their dragons began beating their wings out in the starry sky, seeking higher ground to begin their love play anew.

And still there was Belora, in the back of his mind, sharing the most extraordinary link. She seemed unaware of it, but he knew. Looking into Lars' eyes, he knew too that the other man felt it as well. Astounding. Somehow, Belora was part of them all—part of the union of knight and dragon in a way he was not sure should be possible.

But exploration of that odd thought would have to wait. The dragons were gaining height again as were their passions. The echoes were undeniable as both cocks hardened and lengthened inside their woman once more. This would be a long, supremely pleasurable night. Thinking would come later.

Much later.

Chapter Seven

"I don't want to leave you here, baby." Kelzy paced heavily as she eyed the hut in the forest with disdain.

Jared had taken one look at the sagging roof and took off into the forest. He had come back a few minutes later with some stout branches and silently set to work making repairs while Kelzy argued with her adopted daughter about staying in the forlorn forest cottage all alone.

"I've lived here for years, Mama Kelzy. It's perfectly safe, I assure you."

"That was before that Skithdronian nutcase started riling up the skiths and threatening invasion. What can you do against a hunting pack of skiths on your doorstep, Adora? They'll cut you to ribbons! They're vicious creatures!"

"Some people say that about dragons, you know." Adora's soft voice was cajoling but it didn't work on Kelzy in this mood.

"Don't try to make a comparison between my kind and those spineless, stinking, soulless skiths. They are purely evil, you know. Not thinking creatures at all, which is why that so-called king can herd them about so easily into doing his dirty work. A dragon would never be so easily led. The only thing a skith cares for is blood, carnage, and its next meal."

"And of course, how many heads they can take." Jared came around the back of the small house toward them, shirtless.

Adora took a step back, her eyes glued to the hard male chest displayed so brazenly before her. It had been years since she had confronted her own feminine desires. Frankly she had thought she was well past such desires, but seeing Jared's hard body, sweaty from working to fix her sagging roof and so unconsciously sexy, she felt something long dormant stir to life. In her work as a healer, she had of course seen her share of naked males, and she had been married for several years, but Jared was something different altogether.

This was a knight who trained hard and looked it. He had muscles on top of his muscles and a washboard stomach that made her long to stroke him. Adora became breathless as she watched him move casually toward her, his stride supremely male and confident. The supple ripple of his riding leathers surrounded a cock she was sure was of more than generous proportions. He was a vital male animal, totally unaware of his allure to a woman long denied the pleasures of the flesh.

"Do you like what you see?" Kelzy's voice purred through her mind and she knew the dragon was speaking only to her, well aware of her striking reaction to the gorgeous specimen of man in his prime displayed before her.

"Hush! Please don't embarrass me." Adora flushed hotly, leaning close to Kelzy's flank and speaking in a low whisper she knew the dragon alone would hear.

"It's no crime to enjoy the look of a handsome male, Adora, and my knight is more handsome than most. Look your fill, baby, and remember that if you lived with me he would be your protector. He would keep you safe if you lived with us in the Lair. He would be your family, just as you are mine."

"I can't go back with you." Adora stood from Kelzy's side, her spoken words saying far more than the knight would know. "My responsibility is here and here I must stay. At least for now."

"I don't like it at all, Adora."

"I'll have to agree with Kelzy. Your home is livable, but in disrepair." Jared wiped his hands on his strong, muscled thighs before stretching to put his shirt back on. Adora tried not to watch, but the sensuous ripple of each hard muscle caught her attention. "I've fixed what I can of the roof, but this place won't hold you safe against one skith, let alone a hunting pack. If they come, your best bet will be to run, perhaps climb a tree out of their range. They don't climb particularly well, but you have to be wary of their venomous spray."

"I've seen what they can do. A farmer from the village ran into a feral one last season and was badly burned."

"And yet you still want to stay here? Knowing they may come in force?" Kelzy's voice rose in alarm.

"I must." Adora placed a warm palm on the dragon's knee, stroking comfortingly.

The knight strode to the small pack Kelzy had worn to carry some supplies and things she wanted Adora to have from the Lair. He pulled out a deep brown bundle and handed it to her.

"Take this then. It's a specially treated hide. It's what we make the battle leathers from and it will repel skith venom somewhat. Make clothing for yourself from it. Leggings would be better than a skirt. They'll protect your legs more. Try to cover as much of your skin as you can while still being able to move quickly if need be." He pressed the heavy bundle of leather into her astonished hands. This was a very costly gift and one she knew was not lightly given. "I tried to get some ready-made garments, but we had nothing in your size and there was no time to have them made. I asked them to pick the softest hide we had in the storeroom so it would be easier for you to sew and kinder to your skin. There's lacing and needles inside the bundle too, in case you didn't have what you'd need on hand."

Tears formed behind her eyes and she choked up for a moment, unable to speak. She reached up to kiss his cheek softly, clearly surprising him. With one hand, she held the precious leather and with the other, she pulled him close for a

112

quick hug.

"Thank you, Sir Jared," she whispered into his ear as she pulled back, and then turned to her home quickly so she could tuck away the fabric and gain a moment to regain her composure.

When she came back out, she was more in control.

"He already protects you." Kelzy's voice was soft in her mind.

"Sir Jared, your gift is beyond generous. I will set to work on the garments you suggest this very eve." She tried to make up for her loss of composure with sincere thanks to the man whose thoughtfulness had taken her totally by surprise.

"That's good." He nodded approvingly and held out a cloth wrapped bundle to her. "Kelzy asked me to pack these as well."

She took the large bundle, surprised that it weighed very little. Unwrapping the cloth, the sparkle of dragon scale was bright in her eye.

"What's this?" She looked from the shimmering blue-green scales to the dragon.

"Just a few scales I have shed over the years. We grow new ones, you know, when our scales have been damaged or worn. Our knights save the shed scales to use in shielding or armor, sometimes in weapons. If you incorporate a few of my scales into your clothing in strategic places, they may shield you more effectively."

"Mama Kelzy, I can't accept these. There are fighting knights who need these precious scales, your own included." She looked to Jared who watched with grim interest. She knew he supported Kelzy's decision to give them to her and it touched her deeply. This was a precious, personal gift. Too rare and too valuable to waste on her though.

"Let us do this small thing, Adora. If I cannot be with you, at least a part of me will be. Let me think of you, shielded at least a

*little by my shed scales and my love. Wear them for me, Adora,
so I can fly away with at least some feeling of peace in my heart.
I won't be able to leave you otherwise."*

Adora went to the dragon, touched by her palpable
emotion. Putting her arms around Kelzy's thick neck, she
hugged her, closing her eyes as Kelzy's sparkling wings
enclosed her in a warm embrace. They held each other for long,
long moments.

"I love you, Mama Kelzy."

"I love you too, child. We'll come visit when we can."

Adora realized that Kelzy would bring Jared whenever she
found time away from her duties at the Lair to come visit her.
The idea appealed to her more than she thought it should, but
she let go of that thought as Kelzy pulled away.

"Watch the creatures of the forest," Jared counseled as he
prepared to leave, climbing aboard Kelzy's back with a lithe
grace that belied his huge size. "The animals will know when
skiths are about and the birds will go quiet and fly away. The
game animals flee and even the rodents scurry away. Listen to
them and look to the trees whenever you're outside. Know
which ones you can climb high—at least twenty feet off the
ground. More if you can manage it. Trees with thick leaves may
provide some barrier to venom spray if there are enough leaves
between you and the skiths. Plan ahead, Adora. It could save
you."

She took his words to heart, nodding solemnly. "I'll do as
you suggest, Sir Jared. Thank you once more for the leather
and for fixing my roof."

"I wish I could do more, but I'm not much of a carpenter."

"You managed more in a few minutes than I could do in a
year. Compared to me, you're an expert and I thank you." Her
hesitant smile earned her a return grin from him. It lit his
solemn face and made her feel good for having caused it.

Kelzy turned with him settled on her back, preparing to take off.

"Be careful, child. Your daughter and her mates will come to see you and we'll stop by when we can, but do as Jared says and prepare. War is coming and the skiths will pour over the border first. Beware of them." Kelzy moved farther out into the small clearing from which she would have a clear path to the sky. *"I couldn't bear to lose you again now that I've finally found you. Take care, and if you change your mind, come back to the Lair with Kelvan or pack your things and I'll take you back the next time I visit, all right? Promise me now."*

"I promise." Adora waved to Jared who held up his hand in goodbye. Kelzy flapped her great, sparkling wings and a moment later was airborne.

"I love you, Mama Kelzy."

The clearing was empty and the beautiful blue-green dragon winged off into the sun. Adora was alone.

Newly mated as they were, Kelvan and Rohtina, along with their knights, were given a few days freedom from drilling and patrolling. They made the most of it, flying off to the forest and beyond to frolic and play, mate and explore. Belora went with them, of course, sometimes riding with Gareth on Kelvan's broad back and sometimes with Lars on the sparkling golden Rohtina.

Both men made Belora feel warm and secure no matter what flying antics their dragon partners engaged in, swooping and diving at each other like children. They spent one especially memorable day at the lake where Gareth and Belora had first met, the three of them fucking hard and fast while the dragons mated in the skies above the lake, plummeting to earth to take an unlikely swim in the cool waters as they floated in the aftermath.

They also spent time moving into their new quarters. Lars brought Rohtina's things—shed scales, lots of pretty rocks and gems she had found in her travels and asked him to collect, a few exotic plants, and the oils and potions that helped keep dragon scales supple and shiny. Gareth had similar items from Kelvan's stash and together the two knights organized the small room set aside for the dragons' belongings.

Belora helped settle the men's clothing, taking the opportunity to clean and tidy everything they owned. She repaired the few things that needed it and made note of their sizes so she could begin work on new things for them. She wasn't a terribly gifted seamstress, but it was an occupation she enjoyed and she knew they wouldn't be embarrassed to wear the plain things she could make for them. She also took charge of the small kitchen area, combining the meager stores from each of the knights' previous dwellings and procuring a few things she felt they would need now that she was in residence.

Her mother had taught her how to brew potions and make ointments, lotions, and tinctures. Although she was not a truly gifted healer, she knew the basics and even a bit more than most herbalists. She took the opportunities that presented themselves as they traveled around during those few days to gather some herbs she knew she could use and set up an area in the kitchen where she could work. She made fragrant bathing salts, gentle herbal soaps, and lotions for her skin as well as ointments that could be used to heal most cuts and abrasions, potions and tinctures to keep on hand to cure coughs and colds and other useful items.

She set it all up and knew she would have time when the men were back to drilling and patrolling to do the real work of making remedies for both her own household and to share with the rest of the Lair. She knew that Silla, the older woman who had been so kind to her mother, was the closest they had to a true healer in this new Lair. She would undoubtedly welcome Belora's help and the few potions and cures she could add to the Lair's supplies.

The dragons liked to play in their new, much larger wallow too. Belora and the knights spent a great deal of time sweeping sand back into the large oval pit at the center of their suite, but they didn't mind. The dragons were so happy together, their joy was infectious.

Of course, that wasn't the only thing that passed from the dragons to the knights and their new wife. Several times, Kelvan and Rohtina had flown off to frolic and caught their human partners almost unaware when the mating heat would surge. At such times, Lars and Gareth would come looking for her with such wild lust in their eyes, she knew the dragons were unconsciously feeding their lusts to their partners.

At such times, Belora would feel an echo of the incredible fever the dragon lust inspired and open her arms wide to her two lovers, welcoming them between her thighs and into her soul. They would take her together at such times, both needing to be inside her at the same moment in order to fulfill the dragon lust riding them so hard.

Gareth was speaking with General Jared Armand, Kelzy's partner, when a sudden urge from Kelvan caught him unawares. His dick started to harden and he cursed, looking desperately for a way out. He had to get to Belora, and fast. But first he had to extricate himself from this discussion with his commanding officer.

Jared saw his fidgeting and chuckled. "Dragons giving you trouble?"

"You could say that." Gareth breathed a sigh of relief that his commander was so understanding.

"Get out of here, Gareth. Find your mate." He slapped him on the back and turned away, moving on to another knight who wanted his attention.

Gareth took off at a run for his quarters, praying to the Mother of All that Belora would be there. The knights cheered him as he passed, knowing or guessing what emergency took him so unceremoniously away from the common areas.

When he finally reached his quarters, the pain in his loins was almost unbearable. Kelvan and Rohtina were already joined, rolling and plunging in the way of dragons, high up in the sky, reaching for the sun. Gareth was nearly insane from the pressure.

He loped through the door and began tearing at his clothes even before he reached the bedchamber.

"Thank the Mother!"

Belora was there, already on the bed, with Lars' big cock in her tight pussy, her bare ass facing him...inviting him. Lars saw his friend in the door and moved his hands to spread her cheeks, dropping the small jar of sweet-smelling lotion on the bed near their hips on the way.

Gareth didn't need any further invitation. Freeing his cock from his leathers, he scooped a dollop of lotion onto his fingers, quickly coated his cock, and her. She had grown used to this over the past days and her body accepted him readily enough as he pressed forward, seeking the heaven of her tight ass.

Belora squeaked as he joined her.

"It's just me, my love." He bent to whisper in her ear, finishing with a sharp nip to her earlobe that made her squirm.

"I didn't think you'd make it in time." Her breath came in pants as both men moved in her, driving her lust higher.

"I ran all the way here." He pressed in, feeling Lars' hardness through the thin barrier of flesh that separated them. He also felt the explosion that was nearing in Kelvan's body as the dragons began to reach the limits of their flight. The dragon's lust pushed him, as he knew it pushed Lars, to heights no human male could achieve. It was a gift of their partnership with the dragons that they could reach such peaks and for such long, nearly endless moments.

He felt it coming and knew Lars would go with him when the dragons reached their zenith. It was up to the two human men to make sure Belora went along with them. He used his teeth to nip at her neck while Lars sucked her nipples.

"Now, Belora! Now!" he called, just as Lars bit into her skin and the dragons burst together into the sun. He emptied himself into her ass as Lars' cock pulsed in her pussy, their ecstasy echoing the long plummet to earth of the dragons. It went on and on, holding all of them in its grip while the pleasure wracked their bodies. Belora's climax rolled over her, her inner muscles milking both of their cocks.

Finally, after long, long moments of tight-muscled ecstasy, the dragons began to come back to themselves. They pulled apart and beat their wings just in time to save them from crashing to the ground, releasing their human partners from the rigor of their pleasure. Lars relaxed within her cunt as Gareth felt himself easing in her tight, tight ass. Belora was nearly unconscious from the pleasure and the men settled her between them as they each found the energy to pull back from her luscious body.

Gareth looked down at himself in disgust. He hadn't even managed to undress. His pants were open just enough to release his cock and his shirt was hanging wide, but he had his boots on in bed. Too bad he didn't have the energy to remedy the situation. Later, he thought. He'd get the damned boots off later.

Adora took Jared's advice and spent her evenings sewing a set of clothing for herself out of the incredibly soft leather he had given her. It was the finest hide she had ever owned, and every time she stroked it as she worked, she thought of the tall, strong man who had touched her slumbering heart with the gift. Remembering Kelzy too, she used two of the precious, incredibly strong dragon scales, sandwiched between two layers of hide to make protective soles for a pair of soft boots that laced up her legs and held the leggings close to her body.

The outfit was somewhat indecent, fitting so closely to her skin and emphasizing the curves of her womanly form, but she couldn't resist the soft swish of the leather next to her skin and the warm feel of it between her legs. It reminded her that, although she had a grown daughter now mated and probably starting a family of her own, Adora herself was still a young woman. She had seen only thirty-eight winters and could still have more children of her own, if she really wanted to do so.

She had not even given thought to such ideas. Before meeting Jared, that is. Suddenly, she felt alive again as a woman. She experienced strange feelings in her body that she had not felt in years. Actually, she was not quite sure she had ever felt the way she was feeling at the moment. Jared had awakened something within her that she had not even known existed and she really wanted to see where it would lead, but she was scared.

Jared was not very encouraging. Although he had given her the specially treated leather and been so incredibly thoughtful about her safety, he had given her no outward sign that he was interested in her as a woman. In fact, he had done quite the opposite. He had been polite to the extreme at all times, but somewhat distant. He had not been rude exactly, but not warm either. Still, there was something about the man and his quiet strength that appealed to her. His thoughtfulness was even more attractive, and the fact that he was gorgeous and superbly built didn't hurt either.

She had pants, boots, a shirt and a small head-covering

that would protect her from the worst of a skith venom spray, should she be caught in a dangerous position. Personally she thought she would never need such protection, but she was a practical person and knew well the value of being prepared for all contingencies. Plus, the leather was so scrumptious that she could not resist making a complete set of gear for herself from it.

The design for the clothing was from her own imagination and perhaps a little strange-looking, but very functional if she did say so herself. She had used the precious dragon scales to reinforce certain parts of the outfit like the knees and arms and to add a bit of decoration around the neckline. Kelzy's sparkling blue-green looked beautiful against the soft brown of the hide.

Gareth and Kelvan had dropped in to check on her briefly on their way home from patrolling the border the day before, but she had not seen her daughter for a while. It would be a few days yet until Kelvan or Rohtina were free from their duties long enough to fly Belora and Gareth over for a proper visit, and Adora looked forward to it already.

But today was the day to replenish her herb stock, so Adora found herself on the deer trails in the forest near her small home with a sack of herbs she had already collected, and more to gather. The first inkling she felt that something was wrong was when the birds grew quiet. Since Jared's warnings, she had learned to be even more observant of her surroundings than before. The birds going quiet could mean nothing, or it could be something quite dire. Adora cocked her head, listening, and felt the little hairs on the back of her neck creep up in alarm when the sounds of the forest did not resume after a reasonable amount of time.

Rising slowly, she collected her satchel of herbs and headed quietly for her house. She had enough herbs for one day and the unnatural quietness of the forest was getting to her. Moving as softly as possible, she retraced her steps back to the track just above her cabin, but stopped dead when she saw the huge, brownish slithering tail disappear inside her cabin's front door.

A skith!

And it was in her house. Probably lying in wait for her to return.

Skiths were large, dangerous predators that hunted with cunning, though their mental capacity was nothing like a dragon's. Still, they were formidable foes when pushed into the open. Normally inhabiting the rocky outcroppings to the east, wild skiths did not, as a rule, prey on humans, preferring easier prey like livestock or wild beasts. The new king of the land to the east, however, had pushed the skiths beyond their normal hunting grounds and somehow gotten them to act as a first wave of his army. How he had done that was anyone's guess since skiths could not be reasoned with, yet he had succeeded.

Adora pulled her hood up over her head, well aware that there could be more where that one skith had come from. She wore her new suit of clothes as she had every day since it had been made, but she could not return home. Her only hope was to head for the village. If there was a skith here already, they may have gotten to the village or were heading there. She had to warn the people.

Moving lightly on her feet, Adora skipped through the forest toward the village but on the hill before the small town, she stopped to take stock. She could see even from this distance that the skiths had already been there. Their great bodies had pulled down several houses and the acid stench of their spray drifted on the wind, burning everything it touched that wasn't stone.

The village was empty, the people either dead or long gone, running for their lives. She could do nothing there, she knew. Even worse, she realized as she observed for just a moment too long, a few of the skiths were still there!

One sighted her, and with a deafening scream, alerted his comrades. With a shudder, Adora ran back into the forest, hoping to lose them, but the skiths, though legless, were fast on her track. She ran and ran, but soon realized the skiths would outdistance her easily, closing her in from both sides, and she would be trapped.

Adora thought back to Jared's advice. She had to find a sturdy tree that she could climb. Preferably one with a very leafy canopy that might shield her from at least some of the spray they would no doubt shoot up at her in their hunting frenzy.

There! Just ahead, she found a sturdy oak that reached at least thirty feet or more up into the sky of the forest. Scrambling, she jumped for the first limb and climbed as fast as she dared, out of breath from running but unable to stop even for a moment. The skiths were coming fast now and she had to get out of their range.

Too late, she realized as she felt little pelting impacts against her lower legs and she smelled the unmistakable scent of burning leather. She looked down briefly. Two skiths slithered around the base of the tree, trying to reach up and grab her with their strong jaws, spitting venom as they snarled at her. She looked up and climbed higher. The leather Jared had given her was protecting her for the moment, but she didn't want any more of the venom to hit her. She was not sure if the leather would stand up to a second barrage of the deadly acid.

She settled in the tree as high up as she could go and took a second to look down. More skiths had joined the first two and their writhing bodies tumbled and climbed over each other, trying to extend their reach. She knew they were relentless hunters. They would not give up for days and she did not think she could last more than a few hours clinging to the spindly branches near the top of the tree. The situation was desperate.

Adora closed her eyes and felt tears gathering as she

prayed. She prayed to the Mother of All and then she turned her thoughts to her dear Mama Kelzy. She reached out, as she never had before, and tried desperately to send her thoughts— her final words of love—to the dragon who had been such an important part of her childhood and who filled her heart still.

"Mama Kelzy! If the skiths get me, I want you to know I love you. You are the mother of my heart." Adora's arms started to tremble as her strength and the burst of adrenaline started to fade. *"Tell Jared his leathers worked. He's a beautiful soul and a good man. I'm going to hold on as long as I can and then I'm going to jump from this tree. I only pray the Mother will let me die in the fall so I won't feel anything when the skiths take my head and tear my body to ribbons. Tell my baby I love her."*

Adora returned to her prayers, focusing her thoughts and trying to steady her shaking limbs. There was nothing to do but wait now. She had to hold on as long as possible, and then, she had to end it with what dignity she could.

In the Lair, Kelzy trumpeted distress, her mind panicked, but clear in her orders. She called Jared to her and launched into the air even before he was fully seated. Her distress called to two other dragons as well, her son Kelvan and his mate Rohtina, and their knights soon flanked her wild flight toward the forest.

"What is it?" Jared asked his dragon partner quietly as they flew desperately for the forest. He deliberately included both of the other knights and their dragons in the conversation, linking them the way knights in battle were linked.

"Adora!" Kelzy's voice was panicked, almost irrational. *"Skiths have her surrounded. She's in an old oak tree, but her strength is failing. She doesn't know I heard her! She doesn't know we're coming."*

"We'll get to her in time, Kelz. We must." Jared's voice was

grim and he bent closer to the dragon's neck to reduce wind resistance. Every second counted. *"I want you two to fry the skiths and keep them busy while Kelzy and I get Adora out of that tree."*

"Yes, General Armand. We're with you."

Lars was always the more correct of the newly formed pair and the respect in his thoughts for their commanding officer translated to steadfast devotion, trust, and a willingness to follow their commander, General Jared Armand, and his partner, Lady Kelzy, to the ends of the earth and beyond. Rohtina seconded her partner's words with a roar as Kelvan followed suit. The younger dragons headed a little lower, diving to gain speed as they headed for the location Kelzy shared with them in her mind. They would go in first to occupy the skiths while Kelzy and Jared tried to hover long enough to get Adora.

"We're almost there, Kelz. Try to bespeak her. She might hear you now." Jared used his hands and strong legs to stroke Kelzy's tense shoulders, hoping to offer what comfort he could to calm her so they could act rationally and deliberately to rescue the woman that had become all too important to him in such a short time.

"Adora, child! Hold on. We're coming!" Kelzy's voice boomed through all their minds. She was using all her strength to try to make Adora hear her over the distance that separated them and it was forceful indeed.

"Mama?"

The single word was weak but definitely there. The small group flying desperately closer felt heartened.

"Hold on, child. Jared and I will get you. Hold on!"

"I see her!" Kelvan reported from just slightly ahead of the others. *"It'll be a tough grab, Jared."*

Jared looked over the position of the small woman in brown. He felt some satisfaction as he recognized the leather he

125

had picked out and given her. She had done as he'd suggested and made a rather unconventional suit of clothing for herself. It may just have saved her life, he realized as they drew nearer and he could see the acid streaks on the lower half of her body. He ground his teeth at the thought of her being hit by skith venom.

"I see what you mean. Get to work on the skiths and I'll figure a way to get Adora."

"Yes, sir."

The two younger dragons swooped down through the leafy canopy and soon roars of flame were heard along with skith barking and bellowing. The knights too were employing their slings and even their swords as they got close enough to engage the slithering skiths. Jared left them to it, trying to figure a way to get Adora out of that tree and onto Kelzy's back with him, but it was not possible. She was positioned just wrong in the tree and obviously too weak at this point to move the great distance needed for him to be able to grab her.

"Kelz, you have to snatch her."

"No! I could kill her! It's too dangerous."

Making such a snatch in mid-air would demand all of the dragon's considerable skill as well as unflinching cooperation from Adora. If either of them moved at the wrong moment, Kelzy's dagger-sharp claws could rip her apart.

"It's the only way. She trusts you enough not to move. You have to snatch her out of that tree."

They both heard a disastrous yowl of pain from below. One of the dragons was hurt!

"It's now or never, Kelz. Those youngsters are good, but they can't wipe out the whole nest of skiths down there alone. For that matter, even if we helped, it wouldn't do much good. We need to get Adora out of that tree now. Do it, Kelz. Do it now. She's running out of strength."

Kelzy sent her thoughts to the woman in the tree. *"Baby, I'm going to make another pass and reach out for you with my foreleg. Don't resist and above all, try not to move. Do you trust me, child?"*

"I trust you, Mama Kelzy. Whatever happens, I love you, Mama."

"Oh, baby, I love you too. Hold still now. I'm coming to get you out of that tree. Don't move! Please, baby, don't move!"

Kelzy made the final pass, glad to notice Rohtina was making her way out of the tree canopy, flying awkwardly but still under her own power. She was hurt, but she was clear of the skiths. Kelvan still fought below.

Kelzy concentrated all her effort on reaching out to her human child, snatching her out of the tree without hurting her. She reached out, timing everything as best she could in such bad circumstances and was gratified to feel Adora's waist in her grasp. She closed her talons as gently as she could and felt the small woman in her grasp flinch uncontrollably.

"Adora! Are you all right? Did I hurt you?"

"I'm all right. Thank you for coming for me."

"Hold tight now. I'll have you to the Lair in just a few minutes. I won't let you go, sweetheart."

Chapter Eight

Jared reached over Kelzy's shoulder to look down at the small woman in his dragon partner's grasp. He saw the bright red of blood against Kelzy's blue-green foreleg, but it was hard to discern the jagged scrapes from the dragon's sharp talons against the brown leather that covered the woman.

Pain entered his heart as he saw her pale face, pressed tightly, trustingly against the dragon's muscular leg. She was so brave, so strong. This was a woman of rare character and ability, and she was fast becoming all too important to him. Either way, Adora would not be returning to her home in the forest. Kelzy and he would see to it that she stayed in the Lair.

This was a woman who needed to be protected and given the care she deserved. He wasn't looking for a wife, but he could not let her leave them again. She was much too precious.

"How does she look?" Kelzy's words were for his mind alone.

He didn't want to worry his dragon partner, but neither could he keep the truth from her. *"She's pale and weak. Your talons scratched her and she is bleeding a bit, but she's holding up well."*

"Sweet Mother of All! Why didn't she tell me?"

"It doesn't look too bad, Kelz. Just get us to the Lair and we can fix her up, I'm sure."

"If I hadn't snatched her out of that tree—"

"If you hadn't," he interrupted, *"she would most likely be skith food right now. You did what you had to do and I'm sure*

she'll thank you for it, my friend. You don't hear her complaining, do you?"

"She was ever a thoughtful child. She would never complain, even when she ought to."

"Well, you can nag her about it after we get back to the Lair and the healers have a chance to look at her scratches. She's alive, Kelz." His voice dipped low, surprising him with the deep emotion he felt. *"That's what matters most. She's alive and she'll live with us now."*

"I should never have let her leave in the first place!"

"Neither of us should have let that happen, but we can and will stop her from going anywhere this time. I'll have her bound if I have to."

"We're almost there, baby." Kelzy included all of them in her thoughts now as they approached the Lair. Kelvan brought up the rear with Gareth, both of them keeping close watch on Rohtina's injury as she struggled to fly back to her home.

Jared caught sight of the landing ledge and realized the younger dragons must have sent word ahead, because a contingent of people was waiting for them. Among them was Belora, wringing her hands, with tears tracking down her pale face. Silla, the woman who acted as healer for the Lair, was also there and it was to her side that Kelzy aimed her landing. She hovered a moment, allowing Jared to jump down and catch Adora as Kelzy opened her claws.

Adora was clearly in a great deal of pain, but when she opened her eyes, Jared breathed a huge sigh of relief. She wasn't out of the woods yet, he knew, but she was conscious at least. Just seeing her beautiful eyes blink open reassured him.

"You shouldn't frown so hard, Jared. I'm fine."

"Then why are you only half-conscious?" His gruff voice was for her ears alone as he carried her away from the ledge so the dragons would have room to land safely. Belora was at their side almost instantly, making sure her mother was okay.

"I'm fine, baby," her mother assured her. "Just let me get bandaged up. You should see to Rohtina. She was hurt by the skiths, I think."

Belora gasped and ran for the ledge once more after kissing her mother and assuring her she would check on her as soon as she was patched up. Silla moved closer and lifted the leather away gently and looking at the severity of the scratches. Jared looked too, frowning when he saw the deep gouges, but he stayed silent as Silla made her own assessment.

"It isn't nearly as bad as it looks. A few weeks and she'll be good as new, I think."

Kelzy breathed a warm sigh of relief that washed over them all, bringing a smile to Adora's pale lips. "See? I told you it was nothing."

"Doesn't look like nothing to me," Jared grumbled.

"I can wrap these, but it will have to wait until the more serious cases are tended to." Silla's eyebrow rose in a clear signal to Jared that she expected him to take care of Adora.

"It's all right," Jared answered the demanding eyebrow. "I'll do it. There are others in graver need of your skills." Jared headed for the corridor with Adora still held in his strong arms.

"I can walk, you know," she fussed without much heat.

"I'm not letting you out of my sight until you're patched up and comfortable in bed. In your room. In our quarters." His eyes held hers as he laid down the law.

"Okay." She surprised him by placing her hand at the nape of his neck and stroking him gently.

"You're not going to argue about going back to your forest?"

Solemnly, she shook her head. "After what just happened? The village was destroyed. My patients are all gone—either dead or fled. There's nothing holding me there any longer."

"Well, thank the Mother for that!" Kelzy's disgusted voice floated to them as she followed close behind on their way to her quarters. *"Not about the village—that's terrible,"* she clarified quickly, *"but about you staying with us now. We need you, girl."*

Adora chuckled and closed her eyes, letting her head drift to rest against Jared's strongly beating heart. He liked the way she felt against him, liked the trust she put in him by that simple gesture. Carefully he maneuvered her through the archways and into the room she had used before and placed her gently on the bed.

Kelzy's great head followed them into the small human-sized room to observe that he cared for her girl properly, he supposed. He didn't mind. He loved Kelzy and knew the dragon loved this small woman. They weren't bonded the way he and Kelzy had bonded, soul to soul, but their bond was perhaps even stronger. This was the bond between mother and child, as unlikely as it seemed. The unconventional relationship was just one more reason he loved Kelzy so deeply. She was a special dragon in every way, with a deep compassion and capacity to love that many others of her kind did not seem to possess.

Jared reached for the small buttons on Adora's clothing, undressing her with an efficient hand, over her weak objections. She was almost completely drained of energy. When his hands found the burn marks from the skith venom on her leggings and boots, he marveled at the way her unconventional garments had withstood the fierceness of the attack. When he removed her boots, he noted the hardness in the sole and saw the flash of Kelzy's scales peeping through the burns, shaking his head at her ingenuity.

"Look at this, Kelz." He tossed the boots near to the dragon's head so she could inspect them. "Your little human daughter is a very bright woman."

"Amazing," Kelzy agreed. *"Why didn't we ever think of doing something like this? Incorporating my shed scales between*

layers of treated leather. It probably saved her from some serious burns."

"Definitely. The scale stopped the acid. Even when the first layer of hide failed, the scale and the inner layer of leather were there to protect her. Her skin is unblemished, but the boots and leggings testify to the severity of the venom spray. She was hit pretty badly."

"Hey!" Adora protested when he pulled her leggings clean off, leaving her bare from mid-thigh to her wiggling toes. Jared simply lifted her legs, inspecting her skin minutely for any injury before pulling a blanket from the foot of the bed and tucking it around her.

"Your skin was protected by the leather, Adora. No burns on your legs from the venom, thank the Mother." He looked into her eyes as he reached for her tunic. Her hands came up to stop him, but he brushed them aside. "I have to clean and wrap those scratches." His voice was soft, but his tone serious, and she let her hands fall away so he could do what he had to do.

He pulled off the ruined shirt as gently as he could, knowing by the way her breath hissed that it hurt her, but it had to be done. She was bare beneath the shirt and he was surprised for a moment at the sight of her lovely breasts spilling free of the form-fitting garment. She was built beautifully and quite the loveliest woman he had seen in many long years.

He stroked the side of her face with the backs of his fingers as he noted her discomfort. She was in pain and obviously shy. He had no doubt from her reactions that she had not been with a man since the death of her husband many years before. Jared thought that a crying shame. She was so beautiful, so vital. She deserved to enjoy life and love, not lock herself away in the middle of nowhere where no male could appreciate the beauty of her.

Not that he wanted to be that man, but he saw the value of her and knew she had been wasting her life away hiding in the forest. Here at the Lair, she would be appreciated for the jewel she truly was. He gritted his teeth and tried not to think about all the single men who would be beating a path to her door once they knew she would stay here in the Border Lair. Shaking his head, he concentrated on the task at hand while Kelzy kept the room nice and warm with her puffing breath.

He took a water jug from the nearby table and splashed a bit into the matching bowl, snagging a washcloth at the same time. Slowly and with great care, he cleaned the gouges on her back and side, being as thorough as possible before wrapping a clean cloth lightly around her middle.

Doctoring done, he stood from the bedside and helped her settle comfortably back before tucking the blanket around her. Kelzy stayed just where she was, even after he left the small chamber, and he knew the dragon would watch over her human daughter all night. He shook his head as he reached his own room and tumbled into bed. It had been a long, eventful day.

"How bad is she?" Gareth called to Lars as soon as they landed.

Lars jumped off Rohtina's back and rushed around to examine the damage done to her tough hide by the skith venom.

"Water! We need water here!" Lars began to panic as he saw how deeply the venom had penetrated Rohtina's golden-red hide. It wasn't easy for skith venom to penetrate dragon scale, but there were certain vulnerable areas on their bodies and she had been hit in one of them, just beneath her wing, in the supple crevice where it joined her body. The acid still smoked. Water would counteract that.

Buckets began making their way to her side, a number of knights pitching in to help the wounded dragon. Lars directed them as Gareth helped and Kelvan used his great strength to haul a cistern of water up from the ledge below. He placed it near his mate and the process went much faster as the men could fill the buckets from a nearer source, splashing each one carefully to do the most good.

The ledges were built in such a way that the acid-laced water drained off, over the side of the cliff, well away from any place humans or dragons would come into contact with it. Besides that, the water had weakened the acid to the point where it was more or less safe. It would continue degrading over time all by itself, so the forest below would come to no harm from this emergency drenching.

"Belora, help my mate. I beg you." Worry and pain filled Kelvan's voice, and it echoed through the minds of all present, making a few pause in surprise. Belora moved forward to face the green-blue dragon.

"I don't know what I can do, Kel. You know my healing talent has never been strong. But if I can help her, you know too that I'll do everything in my power to do so."

Kelvan bowed his great head. *"Then go to her. Place your hands on her as you did with me and concentrate. Your power is greater than you know and perhaps the only thing that can save her now."*

Belora looked uncertain, but moved to the golden dragon's side.

Up close, she could see that Rohtina had used all her strength to get back to the Lair. She was badly injured and probably close to death from such extensive damage. The heart she had shown in flying all the way here with no complaint was amazing and Belora felt tears gather behind her eyes.

Gingerly, she reached out and touched the dragon's shimmering golden hide, now burnt brown and black in places, red in others where she bled heavily.

"Concentrate, Belora, as your mother trained you to do."

Kelvan's voice in her mind encouraged her and gave her something to focus on as she gathered the energies that her mother had taught her to recognize, though they never seemed to do what she wished. She had never been a strong healer of humans, but Kelvan insisted that what power she did have felt good to dragons. She had to believe him.

"You can do it, Belora. I have faith in you. You were meant to heal dragons. Not humans. Dragons. You are one of us."

There was no higher compliment a human could receive from a dragon and everyone within hearing distance heard and watched, with varying degrees of awe and suspicion. Belora forced all those watching eyes out of her mind as she focused the energy that was part of her. It leapt to life, as it had never done before, when she touched Rohtina's scarred hide with gentle hands.

Suddenly it was all clear. She knew what she had to do.

Belora placed her palms over the ridges of Rohtina's amber eyes, locking her gaze securely on the dragon's faceted orbs. Belora felt the power flowing through her as never before as she formed the connection with the dragon on several levels.

Belora screamed, feeling just the echo of Rohtina's great pain as her own, but after a moment it began to subside. She felt Lars and Gareth behind her, ready to support her if needed, and her heart filled with love. The love too, transferred to the dragon and reflected back. Rohtina and she joined as one for a breathtaking moment out of time, then the power surged to life within Belora and poured out into the dragon. It went on and on until finally the spell was broken by Rohtina's blinking jeweled amber eyes. They sparkled with life and renewed vitality and a small tear leaked out one side, dropping down onto Belora's elbow, landing there and solidifying into a magical gem.

"Thank you."

Dragons did not cry, but when stirred by great emotion, their magic could release itself in a tear that turned to a precious, magical gem. That Rohtina gifted Belora with the sparkling amber jewel was amazing in itself, but even more amazing was the result of the magical healing. Rohtina was completely well. Not a scratch remained on her previously badly mangled hide. She was whole and healthy once more.

And Belora realized one other little thing that had seeped into her mind while they'd been connected.

"You're pregnant."

Her whispered words were followed by a shout of joy from the watching knights. A dragon pregnancy or birth was always a cause for great celebration since there were so few each year.

"I wasn't sure yet," Rohtina said quietly, the first hint of shyness Belora had ever seen from the magnificent golden dragon.

"Be sure." Belora removed her hands from Rohtina's eye ridges and cupped her rounded cheek. "I felt the presence of the dragonet within you. It is well and happy."

"Praise the Mother of All that you were here, milady. Thank you for saving my mate and my child." Kelvan nudged her with his great head, moving closer to his golden mate.

"It was your faith that made me believe I could, Kel. I've never done that before in my life." Belora laughed now in relief as the dragons surrounded her with their immense bodies and their love and joy.

"Yet it is what you were born to do. Your power is the strongest I have ever felt, even though it's mostly untrained. You were never meant to heal humans, as your mother does. Your power is definitely more dragonish. I felt it that first night you sent your power to me. It's the most amazing thing I've ever encountered."

"It feels pretty amazing to me too, and kind of unreal, but

I'm so happy you're okay, Rohtina." She stroked both long necks and smiled brightly as her own mates came up on either side of her.

"That was amazing." Gareth stopped in front of her and shocked her by kneeling. Lars did the same, grasping her hand and kissing the back of it with his eyes tightly shut against the emotions nearly overwhelming him.

"Thank you, my love, from the bottom of my heart. You amaze me."

"Why are you both down there? Get up." Her amused and embarrassed whisper brought smiles to their faces. She looked up and realized all the knights gathered were now kneeling and offering signs of respect to her.

"What's going on?"

"We honor you, Belora," Gareth explained softly. "It's well known that only those with royal blood have the power to heal dragons. From what we've all just witnessed, we know that you are of the line of Draneth the Wise. Somehow, some way, you are descended of kings."

"No. That's not possible."

"Yes, my love," Lars squeezed her hand. "There's no other explanation. The Mother of All brought you to us in our time of need and now, with you here, we know our cause is just and our mission sanctioned by the Mother herself, for it was She that blessed Draneth and the dragons and brought them together. Just as She brought you to us."

"I can't believe this." Her eyes wandered over the kneeling knights in something like shock.

She swayed on her feet as the rush of energy began to leave her. Lars held tightly to one hand while in the other, she clutched the sparkling golden amber dragon tear. It gave her some energy, but her strength was fast fading.

Gareth and Lars got to their feet and caught her as she

began to lose consciousness. With deep concern, they carried her from the ledge to their apartments. They worried until Kelvan took a moment away from his recovering mate to reassure them.

"The older dragons tell me that after a healing such as the one she just performed, it's normal for the healer to require a day of sleep to recover. Don't worry. She'll be all right tomorrow. It's just draining to do what she did. Plus, it was her first time, so she's not used to the strain. She'll learn to handle the power with more finesse as she uses it. Just let her sleep."

Belora woke over twelve hours later, comfortable in her warm bed. She was naked under the furs with her two mates sleeping on either side of her. Gareth had his hand at her waist, one of his strong thighs between hers as he spooned her from behind. Lars faced her, his arm pillowing her head as he breathed softly into her hair, tickling her ever so slightly with his warm breath.

She looked out into the suite and saw Rohtina and Kelvan snuggling together in their wallow. Kelvan had one blue-green wing resting lightly over his mate and their necks were twined together lovingly. She felt a wave of love pass through her at the sight and realized that her small movements had woken her men.

Lars kissed her before she could even speak. It was a long, deep, hot kiss that spoke of love, commitment, passion, and joy. When he pulled back, he looked deep down into her eyes.

"Thank you, Belora. You saved us all when you saved Tina. I'll never be able to find the words to express—" he choked up a bit and she moved to kiss him, silencing his tumbling thoughts.

"I think I know what she means to you, at least a little. You don't have to thank me. I would do anything in the world for you, Lars, and for Kel and Tina. You all are my family and I love you." She kissed him once more and felt a stirring behind her as Gareth rolled her onto her back and loomed over her.

"And where do I fit into the equation?" The light in his eyes told her he was teasing. He knew full well where he fit in her heart and in her life, but it was good to say the words.

"You're the one who brought us all together."

"Actually, I think that was my role." An amused dragon voice sounded in their heads as Kel brought his great head over to rest in the doorway, watching them. *"After all, I'm the one who found you in the forest, milady."*

Belora sat up and regarded the dragon with some consternation. "What's with the 'milady' stuff, Kel? Why are you suddenly calling me that?"

Kel drew his head up to look down at the trio in the bed. *"Because you are undoubtedly of the royal line. We dragons struck a deal with Draneth the Wise millennia ago and as his kin, you deserve respect."*

"How in the world do you figure I'm related to the king's line? I mean, I know that healing thing was pretty wild, but my mother heals people. What I did can't be all that different."

"Ah, but it is." Rohtina's graceful neck lifted her golden head to rest near Kelvan in the doorway. *"It's a gift of wizards alone and there's no true wizard blood left in this land, but for the royal line."*

Rohtina stretched to rub her sensitive neck scales along her mate's and all three in the bed felt the renewed arousal.

"We can argue about bloodlines later," Gareth grumbled, catching Belora about the waist and tugging her down on the bed once more. "For now, we have more important things to do."

Lars, not to be outdone, pulled her on top of him, using his powerful muscles to lift them both into a sitting position against the headboard of the huge bed. He positioned her across his lap so that she was straddling him while Gareth moved behind her. They felt the dragons withdraw to their large wallow, rolling and twining together as the heat rose between them.

The humans felt the same heat, sharing it with the dragons as Lars tested his mate's readiness with a few teasing, tantalizing fingers. He stopped, his fingers high up inside her, to look deeply into her eyes.

"Tina's pregnant."

"Yes, she is. So?" Her voice was more than a little breathy with Lars' fingers lodged inside her and Gareth stroking her breasts from behind.

"So, you could be too."

Belora gasped as he rubbed that spot right up inside her that always made her squirm. "Mmm. Yes, I could."

"Would you like that? Do you want our baby?" His turquoise eyes sought her gaze, something deep inside, yearning in him. She could feel it.

She leaned forward to kiss him. "I want your baby. And Gareth's. I want a bunch of children with you both."

He sighed as he removed his fingers, caressing her as he moved her into position over his hard dick.

"Then we'd better get to work on them. What do you say?"

"Oh, yes," she breathed as he settled her down over his hard, solid length. He slid home as she writhed on top of him, her inner muscles clenching around him.

She could hear the dragons making a mess of the sand in the central chamber and knew they were nearing completion. It wouldn't be long now before both her men claimed her in perfect union with the dragons that shared their souls.

Gareth pushed her down onto Lars' chest and prepared her rear entrance. He bent over her, biting at her earlobe as he pushed himself home within her tight ass.

"If you have Lars' baby first, I want to be next."

"Yes. Anything, Gareth! I'll do anything you want."

"Now that's what I like to hear." He chuckled as he slid all the way home, the slow and easy passion the dragons were sharing this time having the same effect on the human side of the partnership. "You've had her pussy a lot lately, Lars. I take it you want to plant our first baby?"

Lars began to move in her body as soon as Gareth was fully seated. The men moved in rhythm, driving her wild as they timed their thrusts for greatest impact.

Lars grunted. "If you have no objection."

"Can you two discuss this later?"

The last word rose to a screech as she came hard around both of their cocks and they just kept pumping. She knew then that they'd bring her to orgasm multiple times before the dragons were finished with them. The frantic mating flights of the first few days had settled into long, drawn-out sessions in the sand that were echoed by the humans in hours of love play and the most incredible waves of pleasure she had yet experienced.

"Ssh, Belora, this is very important." Gareth's teeth teased her ear as he pumped steadily into her from behind. "Someone has to make plans here." He stroked her just a little more deeply. "Now what do you think about our first child being fair and blonde like Lars? Or would you rather have a dark-haired tyke first?"

"Either. Both! I don't care!" She sobbed as she neared another peak, even higher than the last.

"Oh, but you must," Gareth chastised her as he rode her through another shattering climax.

"I want..." she panted to catch her breath and her scattered senses. "I want both kinds. Whenever the Mother grants it. I want both."

"Well, if that's what you really want, I suppose that's just what you'll get." Gareth stroked harder, his breath coming a bit shorter now as the dragons neared completion, urging on their knights. Lars too was pounding into her now, stroking her higher and higher still.

"Sweet Mother, Gareth! You're right. Twins!" Lars pushed deeper now, his turquoise eyes bright with both satisfaction and hunger.

"Twins?" she shrieked as she came yet again and still they drove her higher.

"When knight pairs mate with females of the royal line," he was panting, nearer now, "the Mother and Her magic often blesses them with twins." He was close now and she climbed high once more. The dragons rolled furiously just outside the door, grunting and roaring a little as cinnamon smoke filled the air in the slight dome above their wallow. "One from each..." He dug into her as Lars did, both nearing their crisis point.

"Sweet Mother!" Lars swore as he started to come along with his dragon partner. Rohtina's cry sounded through the suite of rooms, followed only a second later by Kelvan's harsh grunt.

Gareth came when Kel did and both knights filled her to overflowing as she screamed their names and convulsed between them. It went on and on as the dragons dragged out their pleasure. Gareth collapsed on them, squashing her for just a few moments between her men, a position she loved. Lars supported them against the padded headboard, his body spasming within her as the pleasure drained from him in long, hot waves.

When they finally found the strength to pull apart and settle bonelessly on the huge bed, Belora thought over what Gareth had said.

"Twins?" Her voice was soft and dreamy. "Truly?"

Gareth reached over to stroke her cheek. "It's more than a possibility. If you're of the royal blood—and I have little doubt you are—then the wizard magic is in your veins. You'll carry one baby from each of us."

"Oh, that would be so beautiful."

"I'm glad you think so." Lars leaned up on one elbow looking down at her, the love in his eyes shining bright in the dim room. "I want a big family. I want our children to have what I never did. I want them to belong to each other and to us."

Belora launched herself into her mate's strong arms. "That's the most beautiful thing I've ever heard." A tear found its way down her cheek and Lars bent to kiss it away. "I want the same thing."

"Then we're all in agreement." Gareth poured wine for each of them from the bedside table and passed the goblets around as they all sat up, some strength returning.

"I didn't thank you both yet for going to save my mother."

"Our children will need their grandmother. Especially when their parents want to spend some time alone." Gareth wiggled his eyebrows and chuckled, making them all laugh.

"No, I mean it. Truly. I didn't think I could love either of you more, but when you put your lives on the line for my mother, I knew that if I lost any of you—human or dragon—I would never be the same. I would never be whole again."

"But what about the king?" Lars spoke softly from the far side of the bed. "You'll have to go meet him and investigate where you come from. The royal blood is too precious to remain anonymous. What if you're a princess? Will you still want to live with us in this backwater Lair?"

She reached over to stroke his stubbly cheek. "Even if I were the queen, I'd never give you up. I love you." She narrowed her eyes in thought. "Though I suppose it is possible that I have strange origins."

"Why do you say that?" Gareth moved up to support her from behind as they lounged on the huge bed.

"It's something Kelzy told my mother. She said that her parents weren't her blood parents, that it was obvious to Kelzy that my mother had been adopted."

"Adopted?" Gareth prompted her when her words trailed off.

"Yes, but she never found out from where, or who her real parents might be."

"By the Mother, then it's more than likely your mother's real parents were of royal descent."

"I guess that could be true." She shrugged. "And twins do run in my family. My mother doesn't speak of them much, but before me, she had twin girls. They were taken just before we moved to the forest when I was about five winters, I think."

"Taken? You mean they died?" Gareth had perked up and looked keenly interested.

"No, they're not dead. At least I don't think they are. They were stolen. It was horrible." She shuddered and leaned into Lars' supporting arm as both men moved closer at the first sign of her distress. "We were in a big town, at a market. Men rushed us. Big men. I remember one had a jagged scar on his face and was missing the two little fingers on his left hand." She shuddered and strong arms went around her, soothing her. "They hit my mother and grabbed my sisters. They were too strong for her and no one would help us. The scarred man tried to grab me, but my mother held me tight and started running. She ran and ran. They pursued us, but didn't catch her. She may be small, but she's fast." A sad smile lifted one corner of her mouth. "After the men left, she tried to find my sisters, but they were gone. We left that day and never went back."

"So the reason she went to the forest, way out in the middle of nowhere was because she was hiding?" Lars puzzled through the situation with his calm logic.

"I never thought of that, but I guess it's true. We didn't have any money and when we came across the cottage, it was empty. No one claimed it when we asked in the village and they welcomed the idea of having a healer nearby. Some of them even helped Mama in the early days, bringing her food and household items to trade for her herbal remedies. That's how we've lived for the past decade and more."

"How old were your sisters when they were taken?" Gareth's voice was calm but very serious.

"I was about five, so I guess they were about ten or eleven."

"Then they'd be in their early twenties now. Twenty-three or so."

"Yes, I guess so." She nodded, settling back into their arms. She saw the look of determination pass between her two mates and wondered at it.

"We have to find them." Lars' quiet voice made her sit up in surprise.

"What?"

"Your sisters. We have to find them. Royal blood is too precious, and women who potentially have the ability to heal dragons and be mates to our brethren are scarcer than even that. We have to alert the other Lairs to be on the lookout for your sisters. Dragons and their knights may be able to sniff them out, now that we know they exist."

Hope entered her heart. "Do you really think so?"

Lars stroked her cheek. "I believe it with all my heart."

"The Mother of All brought you and your mother to us, didn't She?" Gareth sought her eyes, his own smiling softly in the dim room. "Now that we know your sisters could be out there, we'll spread the word. Believe me, there's nothing a knight or dragon likes better than a quest."

All three of them chuckled at that and settled back in the huge bed.

"The Mother did indeed know what She was doing when She brought me to you." Belora's hands snaked out to either side to grasp her mates' hands tightly in her own, her thoughts spinning ahead to the possibility of finding her sisters. The future looked bright indeed.

The Dragon Healer

Bianca D'Arc

Dedication

This one is for the readers who have stood by me for so long, always asking for more dragons! I'm truly honored each and every time someone comes up to me at a conference or writes to me about my books. I couldn't continue to write these stories of my heart without you. Thank you all!

And as always, I dedicate my work to my family, who supported me through several career changes. This last one was a doozy, but they never lost faith in me. I love you, guys!

Chapter One

Silla was a healer. Not the magical kind from fairy stories, but an accomplished apothecary who had trained at the High Temple of Our Lady of Light for many years before being sent out on her journeyman adventure. All healers of the Temple were sent out among the people of various lands for years at a time, to apply their skills in a real world setting. Only after a decade—or sometimes more—as a journeyman would they be invited to return to the Temple and awarded the title of Master.

Silla had at least five more years to go as a journeyman, but she didn't mind. She quite enjoyed traveling the countryside of Draconia, even if she had been given a route on the border with Skithdron. That nation had been causing more trouble of late, and Silla had seen far too many venom burns on people who had been attacked by skiths. Those evil creatures, born of magic during the Wizard Wars centuries ago, were hunters who didn't discriminate in their prey. Anything that moved was in danger around a skith.

They were huge and snake-like, with gaping maws that spit acidic venom. If the venom didn't get you, their multiple rows of serrated teeth would, snapping your head off in one fast chomp.

Luckily, skiths mostly stayed to their side of the border. The flat, rocky terrain in Skithdron was more favorable to their kind. The green, forested mountains of the Draconian border seldom saw a skith incursion—unless they were deliberately herded in that direction. It had been done during the Wizard Wars and a few times since then, but Silla had not been here then.

This new incursion was bad enough that the Draconian King had ordered the creation of a new Lair where fighting dragons and knights would live, train and protect the border. It seemed the skiths' only natural enemies were dragons. Those magical, flying creatures who could breathe fire could also—she had heard—fry a skith in its tracks. It wasn't easy, but they could do it.

Bayberry Heath was one of the small towns on Silla's route. It lay in a protected valley that was as idyllic as it was serene. The town flourished and had a lovely inn as well as several other businesses and shops. Silla always looked forward to the part of her circuit that would bring her to Bayberry Heath, and as she crested the final hill and looked down at the fertile valley, she felt a sense of joy that seldom came to her.

"See that, Hero?" She talked to her horse as if he could actually understand what she said. "We'll sleep well tonight. A bed at the inn for me and a nice stall full of fresh hay for you."

The horse snorted and plodded onward. Perhaps she only imagined that he stepped up his pace when he saw the village in the distance...or perhaps not. She'd come to respect animals and their senses much more since she'd been on the road. The animals of the forest always knew when danger was near or a storm was imminent. By learning to read their signs, she had learned how to protect herself as well.

Her horse, Hero, was old but sturdy, and they'd made a good partnership these past few years. Of course, the Temple had sent her out with little more than the clothes on her back. Part of being a journeyman was learning how to be resourceful. She had earned Hero by healing a wealthy man's wife after a dangerous childbirth. Both the child and the mother had thrived under her care and the man had been so grateful, he'd given her the horse in payment. Silla had wanted to turn him down, but she was frankly tired of all that walking between her assigned villages and farms.

A few months later, another grateful town had given her the cart after she diagnosed the reason behind an outbreak of stomach sickness. The local well had been infested with a particular kind of snail that polluted the water in such a way as to make it seem fine, but sent everyone running for the privy a few hours after drinking. Such a thing could kill the old and the young, but luckily the levels of pollution hadn't reached that critical stage before she had discovered the problem.

Again, she had tried to refuse the cart, but with it, she could make her rounds much faster. That argument, made by one of the villagers, had finally won her over. The headman of the village had spent a few days teaching Hero and Silla how to handle the cart and then they were off to the next village on their rounds.

Silla had soon discovered that the cart made an excellent bed for those nights when she could not find better shelter. She traded for some cloth in the next village and made a pallet of sorts by stuffing the sewn cloth with soft plant fibers and herbs. The herbs kept the summer bugs at bay and made a lovely, fragrant place for her to rest after a long day on the road.

The cart was more than big enough for her and her few things. A short time later, she decided she had space for other wares that she could trade in the villages for better meals and the occasional night at an inn. Silla made many kinds of medicinal potions and even potted a few rare and useful plants that she could barter or give to her patients when needed. Over the past few years, she'd built up a very nice apothecary shop from which the residents of each village could obtain herbal preparations made by an expert hand or even the plants from which they could make their own remedies, depending on the season. But she never charged for medicines or plants when her patients truly needed them. That was the creed by which her Temple lived. Still, she was able to make a few coins from those who were not ailing and traded more often than not for foodstuffs and other items that would help her do her job in more comfort.

Her route overlapped with another, more senior member of her Temple now and again. He would check on her progress in person, in addition to the written reports she sent back every season to the main Temple. Someone there kept track of the spread of illnesses based on journeymen reports and also kept an eye on the journeymen themselves. The accumulation of wealth was not encouraged. Their order was to live simply, but those who were industrious in bringing remedies to the people along their routes even before the medicines were needed were often rewarded with higher positions in the Temple when they returned to become Masters.

Silla was about halfway there now. According to the older healer she'd spent a companionable afternoon with a fortnight ago, she was progressing well. Another five years or so, and she'd be able to return to the Temple with her head held high.

She almost regretted the fact that she'd have to go back. Silla had found that she enjoyed the freedom to travel where she willed. Actually being at the Temple was much more restrictive. Of course, it was better than what her life had been before.

As dusk settled over the valley of Bayberry Heath, Silla topped the last small rise that led down into the village. The innkeeper was already lighting his lanterns to welcome strangers in the night. She could see the little dot of flame dance and bounce as he walked along the gate, lighting the two lanterns on either side of the entrance to his yard that would burn through the night to welcome weary travelers.

It was a sight for sore eyes. And this time, she didn't have to imagine Hero's pace picking up as he probably scented other horses in the stable not too far away. A few more minutes and they'd be there in time for a nice dinner of fresh fodder for Hero and good, hot food she didn't have to prepare for herself. She could almost taste the inn's savory stew. She closed her eyes for just a moment, imagining how good it was going to taste.

Suddenly, an inhuman bellow of unmistakable pain shattered the night. Silla's eyes flew open as she searched for the source of the sound. It had come from up ahead and frightened Hero into a near standstill.

She got him going again, even as she searched the night for whatever had made that tone of pure anguish. If there was any way she could help, she would, but she had no idea what kind of creature could have made such a noise. It wasn't any of the domesticated animals she knew. She'd been called upon to heal a cow or horse more than once and hadn't minded in the least. Her skills were for all things living—person, animal or plant.

Hero balked only once more as they entered the inn yard, and his reasons became clear at once. Next to the inn, on the side away from the horse stables, was an open area filled with sand that Silla had seen before but never questioned. Now she understood why it was there. It was an area set aside for dragons. There was one there now.

It was the dragon that had howled in pain as a big man poured bucket after bucket of water on what looked like deep, acidic burns around the joint where wing met body. Silla winced in sympathy as the creature writhed in pain. Smoke puffed out of his nostrils, but he seemed to be making an effort to contain his agony as the man scurried with the help of what looked to be every able-bodied person from the village.

The innkeeper saw her and came right over, grabbing on to Hero's halter.

"Thank the Mother of All you've come, Healer Silla. If ever there was a need for your medicines, it is now. Can you help yon dragon? We would all count it as a favor. He went down protecting us from a rogue skith and is badly burned."

Silla jumped down from her cart and grabbed her satchel.

"I will see what I can do. Will you take Hero to the stables? Leave the cart in easy reach. There are some plants in back that I may need for the dragon's treatment, if his knight will allow."

"Sure thing, mistress. And thank ye." The innkeeper took charge of her horse and cart while Silla approached the dragon and all the people trying to help him.

Sir Broderick was at his wit's end, trying to help his dragon partner, Phelan, his best friend in all the world. They had been in tight spaces before, but never had Phelan been so injured or in such pain.

They'd fought skiths before and come out unharmed. It had been a lucky—or rather, *un*lucky—shot that had taken Phelan down this time. Thankfully, the good people of Bayberry Heath had been willing to help, getting as much water as they could to bathe the wound free of the terrible acid.

Brodie didn't know what else to do. They'd poured as much water as they could on the burns, bathing the dragon thoroughly. The acid was diluted enough by now to be harmless, draining away into the sand pit beneath them. But Phelan was still in terrible pain.

The shoulder joint on a dragon was one of his few vulnerable places. The acid had eaten deep into Phelan's flesh before they'd been able to land and get water on it. Brodie felt anguish at not knowing what to do to help ease Phelan's pain.

"Sir, I am a journeyman healer from the High Temple of Our Lady of Light. Though I have never treated a dragon before, I offer what help my humble skills may bring to your partner."

The soft voice at his side distracted Brodie for a moment. He turned and stopped in his tracks. Before him was an angel sent from above, a gorgeous woman in the simple clothes of a healer. The marks of her Temple were clearly visible on her cloak, and Brodie thought he'd never seen a more beautiful sight.

"Mistress, we welcome any help you may give." Brodie found his voice after a moment of pure shock. "I confess, I don't know what else to do to ease Phelan's pain. Please help him." That last bit came out on a broken whisper, but Brodie couldn't help it. He had looked back at Phelan while speaking and realized once more he'd never seen his dragon partner in such bad shape. It hurt Brodie to see the great dragon humbled so much.

She started forward even before he'd finished speaking, urgency in her steps, though she approached the dragon carefully. Brodie caught up with her and escorted her to Phelan's worst injury, that in the bend where wing met body.

The healer had pulled a jar from her satchel and uncapped it. Brodie could smell the scent of healing herbs, and he knew the jar contained something that would halt Phelan's pain. That ointment would numb anywhere it touched. Brodie had seen and felt its effects before. This woman could help Phelan. Brodie was sure of it.

Rather than slather on the medicine right away, the healer took a moment to examine Phelan's injury with sure hands. She even bent to smell the wound and used a clean cloth from her pack to dry the area around it as best she could from the dousing the villagers had helped Brodie accomplish.

The moment she applied the ointment, Phelan began to breathe easier. As did Brodie.

"This cream has an anesthetic in it, so the pain should ease," the healer said in a gentle voice.

"Whatever you are doing, keep doing it," came Phelan's voice, filled with relief, in Brodie's mind.

"It's working," Brodie reported to the healer. "He says to keep going."

She continued to work, talking quietly as she ministered to

155

the dragon. "So you really speak to your dragon partner. I had heard tales, but I have never seen a dragon up close before, much less talked to a knight. I have wondered how such different beings managed to work together so well."

"Only men who can hear the silent speech of dragons are eligible to be chosen as knights," he answered offhandedly, watching her treatment of his best friend carefully.

"I see." She examined the wound more closely now that the pain had been masked. "This burn is severe, but I believe we can make him more comfortable while it heals." She turned to address the innkeeper who had returned without Brodie realizing it. "Can you get six burnjelly plants from my cart, please? The biggest ones," she clarified.

The innkeeper scurried off to do her bidding. Brodie recognized the name of an uncommon plant that was highly prized for its ability to heal burns. In the southern part of the country, he knew many housewives and innkeepers liked to keep a burnjelly plant potted and growing on a sunny windowsill if they could get their hands on one. It was a rare thing and something of a miracle that this healer had a supply in the back of her wagon.

She hummed softly while she worked and the sound seemed to calm Phelan. It calmed Brodie too, if truth be told. Between the humming and the confident way she worked to clean and inspect all of his dragon partner's wounds, Brodie felt he was in good hands. Thanks be to the Mother of All.

Phelan had fallen into a light doze, Brodie realized. The prolonged battle, the injury and the pain had wiped him out. The cessation of the worst of his agony had probably allowed the dragon to shut down for a little while and recover some of his strength. Phelan, Brodie had learned over the years they'd been together, had cultivated the ability to take what he called *battle naps*.

He could deliberately sleep, at will, for short amounts of

time that would allow him to stay on duty much longer than most of the other dragons. Phelan had developed the skill while he'd been recovering from the loss of his first knight. Phelan was a dragon in the prime of his life, and even though partnering with a dragon extended the knight's lifetime two or three times over, eventually they still died. When the knight died, the dragon usually went into a period of deep mourning.

Phelan's first knight, Sir Anarik, had died in battle after only a hundred years or so together. He had been one of those defending the old king and his wife when they had been murdered. Phelan and Sir Anarik had gone after the assassins and Anarik had died, leaving Phelan riderless and heartbroken.

Rather than sink into deeper despair, Phelan had set himself the task of safeguarding the remainder of the royal family, in particular the princes, the eldest of whom had become king on his father's death. Roland had been very young when he took the throne, but he had done a masterful job. Attempts had been made on his and his brothers' lives, but Phelan had usually be there to skewer or fry any who tried to kill any more of the royal family.

Which is why Phelan had learned to do without much sleep while on duty. He and another partnerless dragon had devised the scheme and shared the duty of guarding the princes all on their own. They hadn't told anyone, but after they'd conveniently defeated a few would-be assassins, people began to realize what the dragons had done.

King Roland had elevated Phelan, thanking him for his tireless service by making him a member of the Dragon Council and one of the king's most trusted advisors on military matters. When the time had come to build the Border Lair, Phelan had been on top of the list of seasoned warriors who could put the place together.

Brodie had the military and engineering experience to handle such a task. Even before he'd been chosen by Phelan, he'd had the beginnings of a successful career with the specialized group of Guardsmen who assessed the safety of bridges and other public structures. He'd studied building and architecture in some detail as a young man and put that, along with his penchant for warfare, to good use as a military engineer.

His partnership with Phelan had come along quite by accident. A river had spilled violently over its banks, taking out a key bridge during a particularly bad storm. Brodie had been sent to repair the bridge. Phelan had been there to help with the rescue, plucking people and livestock out of the raging torrent and flying them to shore. When Phelan realized Brodie was one of the rare men who could hear him speak, they began to work together to help during the crisis.

After the emergency was over, Phelan hadn't wasted much time in speaking the words of Claim to Brodie and they had been partners ever since. Brodie moved from Guard post to Lair and had begun training in the ways of knights. His earlier fighting experience came in more than handy and his logical mind helped him move up the ranks in record time. He was a strategist and highly trained engineer, which was something the king could well use in his ranks of Dragon Knights and top advisors.

The only thing preventing Phelan from being appointed leader of the new Lair was his knight's lack of a mate. Mated pairs were considered more stable for leading Lairs, so Phelan and by extension, Brodie, were given the role of seconds-in-command of the new Lair.

The innkeeper returned rolling a wheelbarrow filled with potted plants. Sure enough, Brodie recognized the distinctive, puffy stalks of the burnjelly plant from his travels in the south. He took one of the plants as the healer did the same and began snapping off some of the outer stalks and preparing the jelly inside for use.

"You've done this before?" the healer asked in her quiet way.

"I have seen it done," Brodie confirmed. "I can help. I realize you're going to need to use a lot of your supply on Phelan, but I can pay you."

"When there is need, there is no charge," the healer repeated the oft-heard motto of her Temple. Still, Brodie knew many healers made small amounts of money selling medicines in the towns they visited. It was never much, but it probably provided for the occasional creature comfort.

"A noble sentiment. Nevertheless, I will compensate you for the plants. I know how rare they are in these climes."

"I'll let you in on a little secret," she whispered with a mischievous expression, leaning toward him.

She smelled of lavender and lilies and warm woman. A heady combination that made him want to lean closer and breathe deeply. She was a gorgeous creature and now that Phelan was resting more comfortably, Brodie saw again what he'd seen when he first beheld her. This healer was a beauty with a gentle touch and an attractive scent. He wanted to kiss her, but he knew that would be entirely inappropriate at the moment. Still, if the opportunity presented itself later, he wouldn't be shy. He wanted to see if she tasted as sweet as she smelled.

"If we only use the outer stalks," she went on, oblivious to his carnal thoughts, "the plant will survive to grow more in time. Even trimmed as these will be when we are done, I can earn a few pennies with them from the villagers to pay for my room and board." She smiled and leaned back, snapping another of the outer stalks off her plant and cutting it open. "So you see, I will not be out much from helping your friend. To be honest, I am honored to assist a dragon and knight of the realm."

"You honor us with your skill and willingness to help, healer," Brodie replied politely. "I'm Sir Broderick, but my friends call me Brodie. What's your name?"

"Silla," she replied softly, almost shyly.

He wondered how a lovely, attractive and obviously skilled woman had ended up in such a lonely occupation, but he would not pry. Not yet. Soon though, he vowed to know all her secrets.

"You are lovely, Silla." Brodie wondered where the restraint he usually practiced in his words had suddenly gone. He hadn't meant to blurt out his thoughts like that, but she seemed to be blushing in the dim light of the torch-lit courtyard.

No coy court games for this beauty. No, she was more genuine and unpracticed in her responses. Shy. Beautiful, soft-spoken and shy. Brodie never would have expected it of an obviously successful journeyman healer. To be on the road by one's self took a strong character and usually meant the traveling healers were much surer of themselves and somehow...brasher. But this woman could still blush.

Brodie found himself enchanted by the puzzle of her.

Chapter Two

Silla was flattered and somewhat uncomfortable with the knight's attention. She didn't know how to reply to his words. Few men had ever made such dramatic statements to her. Most saw her as a healer first, woman second. If at all.

She busied herself with preparing the plant stalks she would need to treat the dragon. Reaching into her satchel, she retrieved one of a set of small bowls she often used to mix herbs. It would do as a vessel to hold the jelly as she worked. She began scraping the jelly out of the cut stalks into the bowl. The knight followed suit, bending close to her as she worked.

He was so tall. And younger than she was, if she didn't miss her guess. His dark curls made her fingers itch to touch them and see if they were as soft as they looked. He had brown hair kissed with streaks of gold, cut short in the warrior fashion, but curly in the most attractive way. It was windblown from his flight here, no doubt, and soot covered his clothes and made a stripe across one cheek.

He smiled at her, a question in his eyes. "Is there something on my face?"

Drat. She'd been caught staring.

"Yes." She was forced to explain her fascination with his handsome features. "Soot, I believe," she answered quietly.

"A hazard of working with dragons." He chuckled and surprised her by leaning closer, offering his cheek. "Could you?" he asked with seeming innocence, but he had a devilish smile on his face.

Silla decided to take up his challenge. Daring greatly, she

took a clean cloth from her satchel and wiped at the gray mark along his cheek. The rasp of his beard stubble made her insides quiver and she damned the layer of cloth between her fingers and his skin. She wanted to feel the heat of his body, the bristles on his cheek.

It was irrational. She hadn't ever wanted another man since the dissolution of her disastrous marriage. She thought she'd been forever cured of the yearnings she'd once known as a younger woman. Yearnings that had been demolished and replaced by the repulsion she'd learned in her painful marriage bed.

But this knight…he was different. He made her feel things she hadn't dreamed of in too many years to count. He reawakened something in her that wanted to know more. Other women seemed to enjoy bedding their mates. Many talked to her, in the course of her duties as a healer, about the intimacies of the bedroom. She'd come to realize that not all husbands were oafish brutes. Some were tender and loving with their wives. Some lovers were also overly playful and got into mischief that required her services to heal.

She knew all this with an academic sort of viewpoint, but she'd never imagined she would want to know the touch of a man again. Not until meeting this amazing, alarming, disarming knight.

The soot on his cheek was long gone, but the moment held. Their gazes locked and his head dipped lower, closer to hers.

A clang out in the yard made her jump and the moment was broken. She looked over to see the innkeeper ushering the last of the townsfolk into his common room. There were many who had joined in the bucket brigade to help the dragon. They were all now enjoying a drink. She had heard Brodie—Sir Broderick, she reminded herself sternly—make the offer of a round of drinks on him by way of thanks as the last of the buckets was emptied.

Silla looked down at her hands and saw there was enough jelly in the bowl to at least begin treating the dragon's burns. The sooner they got the jelly on the wound, the sooner the burns would start to heal.

She moved away from the disturbing knight and closer, once again, to the dragon.

"There is another bowl like this one, in the first pocket of my satchel," she said without meeting Brodie's eyes. Blast! She had to remember to think of him as Sir Broderick. Brodie was much too familiar for a knight of the realm. "If you could continue preparing the jelly, sir, I will begin treatment."

She heard a sigh and then movement behind her as the knight reached into her pack, which was lying on the ground. She observed him finding the second bowl out of the corner of her eye as she scooped a handful of the jelly out of her bowl and began dabbing it gently on the dragon's wounds.

She began to hum a healing chant as she worked, using light strokes on the dragon's raw flesh, making certain every last inch of the damaged areas were covered. She ran out of jelly quickly, but Brodie—Sir Broderick—proved an excellent assistant, handing her a full bowl when hers emptied. They repeated the dance quite a few times before all the dragon's burns were treated.

When she turned back to the area he'd been working in, she found all her potted plants well pruned with the growing centers intact. The plants would live to grow new stalks. He had been listening. She smiled in satisfaction. A man who really listened was a rare and wondrous thing in her experience.

"That should do for now." She rubbed the excess burnjelly off her hands with a small square of cloth. "We should leave the wounds open to the air tonight. Do you think he can sleep in this position? If he rolls and gets dirt in the open wounds, it would be bad." She looked over at the dragon's head, surprised to find his eyes open and his head turned to look at her. "Well,

163

hello there, Sir Dragon. I hope you are feeling better than when you came in." She bowed low, holding the dragon's gaze. Everyone who was sent into Draconia by the Temple was given instruction on how to deal with dragons should they cross paths with one. There was a certain etiquette to be followed.

"I feel much better. Thank you, healer. I will sleep now and not move from this position. I am comfortable enough."

The great head turned and settled on the dragon's front leg, his eyes closing. Silla was still shocked immobile by the sound of the dragon's booming voice inside her head. Never had she imagined such a thing, but there could be no doubt. It was the dragon who had spoken to her, silently, in her mind.

Silla shook her head as she gathered her supplies and put them in the wheelbarrow with the now much smaller plants. She passed the knight as she did so, knowing she had many chores to see to before she could rest this night.

"Your companion will require further treatments," Silla told the man. "I will prepare the jelly tonight and apply it at first light, if that is all right with you, sir." She kept busy while she talked to him, mentally taking stock of what she needed to do before going to sleep and the subsequent dawn.

A hand on her forearm stopped her when she would have lifted the handles of the wheelbarrow. She looked up to meet the gaze of Sir Broderick. Brodie.

She was caught in his gaze. He was closer than she had imagined. Closer and far handsomer than any man had a right to be. She felt breathless again at his proximity.

"Allow me," he said in a quiet voice as he lifted the wheelbarrow and waited. It struck her that he was waiting for her to direct him.

"You're very kind, sir." She knew she was blushing as she led the way toward where her cart was parked next to the stables. There was a water pump nearby and an empty trough that would serve her purposes. She had to clean the implements of her trade and prepare them for tomorrow before she could seek her bed.

Much to her surprise, Sir Broderick did not leave after delivering the laden wheelbarrow. He had placed it alongside her cart so she could move the now-bare plants into the covered storage area with the rest of her stock. At the same time, she removed four plants that still had all their stalks and put them into the wheelbarrow with the two empty bowls they had used before, plus two more bowls she retrieved from the back of her cart.

Brodie—make that Sir Broderick—stayed by her side and picked up the wheelbarrow once again when she moved toward the empty trough. She got there first and began pumping water into the basin. She didn't need much. Just enough to wash her implements and her hands.

She realized then that Sir Broderick's hands were probably still covered in the slimy jelly.

"If you want to wash your hands first, I'll pump the water for you," she offered.

He looked like he wanted to argue the point, but gave in after a moment's consideration. "I would be much obliged."

Brodie—no, she must think of him as Sir Broderick, lest she slip and become far too familiar—moved close, washing his hands briskly. He was so large, and so near. He had been through battle, injury and his dragon's pain today and he still seemed so strong and vital. Because the pump was small and the space limited, she couldn't help but stand very close indeed to his tall, muscular form. Even in the flickering light from the lanterns all around the inn's yard, she could clearly see the masculine lines of his angular jaw, straight nose and strong chin. He was really too handsome for his own good. For her good too.

She tried to avert her gaze downward, but that brought her focus to his thickly muscled arms, rippling as he moved. She lowered her gaze even more and was caught by the sight of his strong thighs, encased in black leather that followed his form so faithfully. Her mouth went dry at the sight.

Then she noticed the tear in the soft hide of his pants. And the blood.

"You're injured," she whispered, shocked he hadn't been limping or even once complained of the discomfort he must be in. She could readily see the angry red gash along his right thigh. It looked deep and very painful. She had seen such wounds before. She knew what they did to a normal man. That this brave knight was still standing and acting as if nothing was wrong, was a testament to his fortitude.

"It's just a scratch," he replied, glancing down at his thigh and shaking his head. His nonchalant attitude amazed her.

"That is more than a scratch, my lord." Normally she would not have argued the point, but perhaps, she admitted within her restless mind, she wanted to prolong this encounter. She didn't want to leave his presence yet. His wound was a fantastic excuse for her to spend just a few more minutes with him.

"I will wash it when I get to my room." He shrugged, as if it were of little importance. "Let me help you get set for the morning first. I want to help in whatever way I can, since you are being so kind and generous aiding Phelan."

"It is my honor and my duty, milord," she replied, slightly embarrassed by his praise. "But if it will get you off that leg faster, by all means, let us get down to business. This will not take long. And then I insist on dressing your leg wound. It will not help your dragon if you fall from an infection that could have been easily avoided."

He smiled then and her breathing faltered. He was potent at close range. He was incredibly handsome—why couldn't she stop thinking that?—and seemingly unaware of his effect on a female's ability to think clearly in his presence. With slightly addled wits, she changed places with him and allowed him to operate the water pump. She cleaned her tools and her hands as quickly as possible, wringing out the small cloths she had used that were not that soiled. She would let them dry overnight. The cloths that were truly dirty, she segregated into a small pile for later attention.

For the next ten minutes, they worked companionably, cutting the outer stalks off the new batch of plants and preparing the jelly for tomorrow morning. Burnjelly was more potent when it had between twelve and twenty-four hours to set before use. This batch would be even more helpful to the dragon in the morning as long as they were careful to cover it securely overnight.

They sat on the edge of the half-empty trough, each working silently at first. They worked well together, establishing a rhythm. Brodie—Sir Broderick—was good company and did not balk at work, even while injured. She was more impressed by him the more she was around him.

"So tell me, how did you come to the Temple?" Brodie asked out of the blue after they had been working for a few minutes.

She was so surprised by his question, she almost dropped her knife into the trough. Regaining her balance, and her equilibrium somewhat, she thought about how to answer his question. It was a loaded one, to be sure.

Chapter Three

"It is a long story and a sad one for the most part," she said finally, deciding to give him a little bit of the truth. "I was married off young to an old man. When he wanted to be rid of me, he beat me and threw me out into the street. A kind-hearted soul called one of the brothers from our order and he treated me. It was a long recovery and over the time I spent in the Temple gardens, I discovered an affinity for plants. They allowed me to stay on and join the order to train as an apothecary. As you can see, I made it through to journeyman." She shrugged, gesturing toward her cart.

"How long have you been on the road?" He seemed to understand more about the way the Temple worked than most people.

"About five years. I'm almost halfway through my journeyman trial."

"You have done very well for yourself." He gave an approving glance to the cart and her stock of rare plants.

"You seem much more familiar with the Temple and its ways than most people I come across. How is it you know so much about the order?"

"We knights meet many people on our journeys, but as it happens, someone dear to me is a member of your order."

"Truly? Do you think I would know him?"

Sir Broderick gave her a secretive smile. "Oh, I would bet you know him if you spent any time at all in the Temple gardens. Have you met Brother Osric?"

"Osric? He is the best of us. The leader of all apothecaries in our order."

"He is my brother," Brodie said in a playful voice, as if sharing some private joke, but she didn't quite understand. It was becoming increasingly difficult to think of him as *Sir* Broderick when he was so open and warm. The shortened version of his name fit his friendly manner, and she knew it was a losing battle to keep that more formal distance between them in her mind.

"That's not possible. He is probably old enough to be your father," she said with a scowl of confusion.

"A benefit of joining my life to a dragon's." Sir—make that Brodie—glanced toward the sandy area where the dragon lay sleeping. "I will outlive my baby brother, Osric, by many years. Perhaps a lifetime or two." He shrugged, but she saw the discomfort of that knowledge sitting restlessly in his eyes, even in the flickering lantern light. "I was chosen by Phelan when I was the age you probably are guessing me to be. In truth, I've lived double that time already, even though my body stays as youthful as it was when Phelan gave me just a tiny portion of his magic."

"I have never heard of such a thing," she admitted, allowing some of the awe she felt to be heard in her tone.

"It is not widely known, though it isn't a secret, exactly. So few men can be knights, it isn't something that regular folk seem to concern themselves with."

"So you're really older than me, though you look younger," she thought out loud. Only after she realized what she had said did the blush start in her cheeks.

He sent her a speculative glance. "Indeed, mistress. I am far older and wiser than a pretty young thing like you." He chuckled, leaning forward to place the plant he'd been working on in the nearby wheelbarrow. The action brought him closer to her and for a heart-stopping moment, she thought perhaps he meant to kiss her.

The disappointment she felt when he didn't was involuntary, but all too real. She'd only just met the man and already, she wanted to feel his kiss.

She wanted even more than that, if truth be told.

"Living so long must be a blessing indeed," she said, speaking quickly to cover her confusion. She hadn't really thought through her words and the way he looked at her made her realize their folly. It was not a gift to watch one's family grow old and die. "Forgive me," she added, looking down at her work, embarrassed yet again by her reactions to this confusing knight.

The back of his fingers touched her cheek, then her jaw, so gently. It was like a butterfly's caress. A strong butterfly that urged her to look up and meet his gaze. She complied, feeling much like a young girl, quivering at such an innocent caress.

"I can never regret joining my life to Phelan's. He is my best friend," he said simply. "But all knights search for a family of their own. We know we will eventually lose the family we were born to when we are chosen. It seems a small price when you consider the amazing benefits of partnering with a dragon and being able to train and fight to protect our land and our people. It was my life's ambition to become a knight and I was never happier than the day Phelan first spoke the words of Claim upon me." He withdrew his hand from her face, but held her gaze. "But I will always search for the woman who can complete our circle."

That sounded serious. And why was he looking at her so speculatively all of a sudden? Could he possibly think she was the woman he seemed so determined to find? She felt breathless once more, but then she recalled the strange things she had heard about marriage in dragon Lairs.

She stood and shook a bit of dirt that had fallen from one of the plant pots off her skirt. It was as good an excuse as any to put some distance between herself and this confusing man.

"And by circle, what exactly do you mean?" She walked over to her cart for something to do, pretending to need something out of the back.

She was unprepared to feel his hard warmth at her back, his hands on her shoulders. She was up against the wheel of the cart, reaching over the waist-high side when he trapped her with nothing more than his heat and his light touch on her neck. Just one finger. Stroking. Raising goose flesh with the slow, back-and-forth motion against the sensitive skin just under her ear.

"Phelan is an older dragon," he said, confusing her yet again. Although it was probably his touch that made every last brain cell she owned jump around in mixed delight and panic. "He has a mate. She is named Qwila and her knight is called Geoff. He was chosen only about a decade ago and is probably about your age, maybe a bit older, if that makes any difference to you." That tantalizing finger moved to trace her ear and her insides quivered while her body shivered. "When one of us finds the woman who can complete our circle, only then will Phelan and Qwila be able to join once more in a mating flight. Until we have a woman of our own, Phelan and Qwila must abstain. Don't you feel sorry for them?"

He chuckled lightly and she felt the soft whisper of his breath against her ear, increasing her shivering.

"I guess so," she answered, not really understanding what she was responding to. She'd lost the thread of his conversation somewhere along the line. His touch was too distracting. Too arousing. Too amazing.

He moved away slightly, both hands dropping to her shoulders. With gentle urging, he turned her to face him, her back against the side of the cart.

His head dipped lower. Slowly. So slow, she could easily have objected, but she found herself powerless in the face of his advancing ardor. She wanted his kiss. Now, more than ever, as he'd worked her into a small frenzy of need with that simple, stirring touch.

His mouth met hers and she slipped happily under the waves of his desire, awash in sensation she had never felt before. Not once in her life had she felt so aroused by a kiss.

Her opinion of sex was undergoing a startling revision as Brodie taught her about passion. Flaming, brutal, enslaving passion. All with a simple kiss. His hands remained on her shoulders, only his mouth claiming hers, taking possession.

His taste was divine. Hot. Carnal. Manly. He was temptation itself, daring her to go farther, to follow him into the flames of perdition. Silla was lost. Brodie was her anchor in a whirlwind of chaotic pleasure. Her guide and her teacher. Her salvation.

When the kiss ended, it wasn't because she drew away. No, Brodie had stepped back, and belatedly Silla heard the loud bang of a metal bucket inside the stable, not far from them. The stable boy, no doubt, was seeing to his charges and the noise had probably reminded Brodie they were not necessarily alone.

Silla was grateful he'd stopped before anyone saw more than what had been, after all, just a kiss. She had a reputation to uphold in this town. She had to be circumspect in all her dealings with men, lest they get the wrong idea about her. Respect was important to a healer's success. If the people you treated had no respect for you, they would seldom listen to your advice. It had taken a long time to prove her worth as a healer to the people along her circuit and she didn't want to ruin that hard work with idle gossip about her willingness to succumb to a handsome young man.

"Sir Phelan should be good for tonight. He said he wouldn't move out of position, which will help the wound heal more cleanly."

"Wait. You could hear him?" Brodie stopped in his tracks, but she wasn't going to be waylaid. She wanted to get inside, away from temptation.

"Well, of course. It was a first for me, to be sure, but he talks to you every day, doesn't he?" She didn't wait for an answer, not looking at him as she gathered her things.

Moving briskly, she turned away from Brodie and bustled around the wheelbarrow. She put the bundle of dirty laundry into her cart along with the now much-smaller plants. The oilskin cover she used to keep the back of her cart dry in rainy weather went over the top, securing everything for the night. The delicate plants would keep well under the cover if the temperature dipped too low for them.

She couldn't look at Brodie as she finished her preparations for the morrow, but she felt his silent presence there. Watching her. Probably waiting for some sign or trying to figure her out. She wished him luck with that. She couldn't even understand her own motivations or responses at this point. Sir Broderick and his devastating kiss had her in a dizzying storm of confusion.

But what lovely confusion it was.

Dare she turn to him and let the passion he inspired consume her? Silla had trod a safe and narrow path for so long, she wasn't sure if she still had it in her to be daring.

"I take my leave of you, Sir Broderick," she said formally, dropping a small curtsey, unable to meet his gaze.

"I will see you to the inn," he said softly, taking her arm and moving them forward, toward the wide front door of the well-lit common room. "And don't you think you should call me Brodie? If anyone in this village is entitled to such liberties, it is you, my dear." His teasing tone made her look up at him as they walked quietly across the large inn yard.

"Brodie, then," she amended, finding that little spark within that wanted her to jump headfirst into this man's arms and not look back.

His grin teased her and made her steps falter, but they continued their slow progress across the well-trod yard. She realized then her scandalous behavior. She had kissed the man as if there was no tomorrow and they had only just met. The thought made her pause. It made her wonder if she was just one in a long string of conquests for the handsome knight.

Brodie must have read something of her mood in her response because he stopped their progress and turned her to face him.

"Just to be clear, milady, I do not go around kissing every pretty lass that crosses my path. Tonight has been unique in many different ways and I am not too proud to admit that Phelan's condition has put me off balance." His deep brown eyes begged for understanding and showed just a tiny bit of the vulnerability he was feeling with his dragon partner laid low with such a grievous injury.

Silla's soft heart thawed. "I did not wish to be one of many, my lord," she answered honestly.

"My dear, you are one in a million. Exceptionally unique. Never to be duplicated." His smile lit her world for a brief moment.

She turned back to the inn, her heart filled with joy. Lantern light spilled out the windows and music could be heard wafting on the night breeze. They spoke no more as he opened the large door for her and they discovered the locals were having an impromptu party. It didn't show any signs of stopping and nobody noticed them standing in the darkened doorway. The innkeeper and his staff were being run off their feet by demands for food and drink.

Silla felt every bit of her weariness. It had been a long day on the road and then treating the dragon and meeting his knight who disturbed her peace on so many levels. She was bone-weary and didn't want to have to battle through the crowd to get the innkeeper's attention, much less have to haggle with the man for room and board.

"It is busier than I thought in here," Brodie spoke in a low voice, next to her ear. "Is your room already settled?"

She shook her head no, feeling tears threatening. Tears? She didn't know why she was so emotional. She had been walking this path now for five years. Her patients must be seen to before her own needs, but tonight she wished—as she had a few times before, in weak moments—for someone to help her. A partner. A friend. Someone to help ease her path in life as she tried to ease the way for others. Sometimes it felt like the weight of the world had settled on her shoulders and she had to hold it up for everyone else.

Sometimes—in the darkest hours of the night—she prayed for someone to help hold up that heavy weight on her shoulders. Someone to help her as she helped him.

But she knew from bitter experience that having a man in her life was no guarantee of such things. She had hoped for a good friend. Perhaps a lover. Even a pet could help ease some of her load. In fact, she had renamed her horse Hero because he was, in his own way, her hero. He had come into her life at a time when she had grown too tired and weak to walk from place to place. The healer had become sick of walking and her Hero had arrived to carry her where she needed to go, giving her time and energy to heal herself so she could continue to heal others.

"There is a special room always kept ready for patrolling knights," Brodie told her. "The entrance is on the outside, very near the sand pit so we can be near our partners. There are two beds in the room. You could share it with me," he offered.

Chapter Four

Silla turned to look up into his eyes. She saw no trickery in his bottomless brown gaze, though the firelight brought out lively flecks of gold in his otherwise pure brown irises.

"I am weary to my bones," she told him honestly. "If you expect more than to simply share the room, I will seek shelter elsewhere."

"I am a knight and a gentleman," he protested, but with a gentle smile that said he understood her caution. "You have my word I will not molest you in the night. On the contrary, I will protect you. Especially since you are the purveyor of burnjelly to heal my dearest friend in the world." He winked at her, and she caught his humor. He really did seem to be a nice man.

"Then I will take you up on your offer, relying on your discretion. My reputation is all I have and I would not lose it lightly." She looked around at the gathered villagers. Many were well on the way to intoxication and nobody seemed to notice her standing by the door.

"I understand, milady. Your honor will come to no harm from me," he promised.

She followed as Brodie led the way out the door and into the flickering light of the lantern-lit yard. They retraced their steps back toward the dragon wallow and up to a small door built into the side of the inn. Sure enough, when he opened it, there was a bedroom. Large by inn standards, it was comfortably appointed. Not too fancy, nor too plain. It was large enough for two big knights and their gear to bunk down comfortably.

One thing she did notice, though, was that one of the beds was built on the enormous side of large. The other was clearly a single bed. She put her cloak and the small pack she'd taken from her cart on that one, but Brodie seemed to notice her confusion as he sat on the much larger bed and smiled at her.

"This bed is built for married knights and their lady. The other is for when single knights patrol together. The senior of the pair gets the larger bed and the junior has to make do on that." He pointed to the small bed behind her.

"It will do well enough for me," she countered, feeling weary again. She turned away, releasing her outer robe. She caught it before it fell to the floor and draped it neatly over the chair that stood beside the smaller bed.

She felt the unnerving caress of Brodie's gaze as she took off as much of her outer garments as she dared. She would sleep in her dress. She had done so before and was used to it.

A sudden thought struck her as she sorted through her small pack. "I'm sorry. I forgot all about your leg injury. Shall we tend to it now?" She picked up the other satchel that held her emergency supplies. She never went anywhere without that well-worn bag.

"I told you, it's nothing."

"Please allow me to be the judge of that. Take off your pants and lie down."

"Now that's what I like to hear." Brodie's eyes twinkled up at her, and she had to laugh.

She took out an oilskin and towels to put under his leg so they wouldn't soil the bed linens with his blood. She'd have to clean the wound first and for that she brought over the basin and water pitcher she found waiting on a small table by the door. The water was fresh, she noted from its smell, and the basin would suit her purposes. She poured a small amount of water into the basin and added cleansing herbs that would ensure his wound was disinfected and the pain dulled somewhat.

When she returned to the bed, he'd complied with her request. He was dressed in a simple shirt that hung past his hips. He had to have had the tunic on under his leathers, but she hadn't noticed it before. He'd shed his leather riding gear, including his jacket, boots and pants, and his long legs were bare to her inspection.

She used a small square of clean cloth, dipping it into the water that had turned a pale yellow as the dried herbs released their healing properties. In her line of work, she went through a lot of linen and had to keep her satchel full of clean cloths, bandages, towels and rags at all times. She had restocked her supply from the back of her cart without thinking, but was glad of it now. The wound was deep and had bled quite a bit.

Silla tried not to think about the muscled legs with only a dusting of hair. She had worked on many male patients before, but none had elicited this kind of feminine response from her. She felt a little shaky as she approached him, the cloth in the basin she carried. She sat on the side of the huge bed, putting the basin at his side.

"Can you hold this steady?" she asked perfunctorily, not even waiting for him to take hold of the rim of the basin before reaching for the wet cloth. She rung it out a bit, then went immediately to work on the wound.

She tried to be as gentle as possible, but she saw the way his leg muscles clenched when she probed.

"I'm sorry, but the wound must be as clean as possible before infection can set in. I'm surprised you were walking on this for so long." She worked carefully but steadily, using a towel to catch the bloody water. "The herbs will disinfect and numb the area. It should not hurt so much in a minute, once the effect takes hold."

"It feels better already, Silla. Don't worry. I've had worse and lived to tell the tale."

She knew the truth of that just by looking at the collection of scars on his legs. Some were old, some new. Many were bigger than the one he would gain from this injury. They told a story of life hard lived. A body that was used to fighting and hard work...and war.

Silla didn't comment as she continued her work. She used all the treated water before she was satisfied the wound was indeed clean enough. He'd stopped flinching early on, thanks to the anesthetic in the water, and she'd been able to get to the bottom of the cut to see that it wasn't as deep as she'd feared at first glance.

"You don't need stitches, but I will bandage this for tonight, to keep the skin in place while it seals. By tomorrow, you should be able to do without the bandages as long as you take it easy." She applied a special salve she had made for such injuries while she spoke, then wound a clean length of bandage around his leg with his assistance.

He lifted his leg enough for her to get underneath. Removing the soaked toweling gave her more room to work, but the cut was high up on his thigh and every trip around the circumference of his thigh brought her in close proximity to his cock. Which was hardening with every revolution of the bandage.

Silla tried not to notice. Some men responded to a healer's touch whether they wanted to or not. Somehow, though, she didn't think Brodie was the kind of man to respond to just any woman's touch. No, the hardness so poorly hidden by his tunic hem and trews was most likely just for her. Especially after that amazing kiss they'd shared in the yard that had left her shaken, stirred and altogether too aroused for her own comfort.

"I would say I was sorry, but I'm not." He must have noticed the direction of her gaze. She felt heat flood her cheeks as her gaze shot to his. He was smiling, but this smile held an ocean of knowledge. A sea of desire.

Dare she dip her toes into the water?

"This sort of thing happens with male patients sometimes." She tried to sound nonchalant, shrugging it off.

"I don't think I like the sound of that." His expression suddenly changed from amused to angry...and possessive? How could he feel possessive of her in so short a time?

"It is a hazard of my profession nonetheless."

He made a sound in between a sigh and a growl that wasn't hard to interpret. Amazingly, he was jealous.

She looked up at him, confused, oddly flattered and—she wasn't too proud to admit—aroused. Again. Still. She wasn't sure which.

Brodie was everything she'd dreamed of in a man and never really thought existed. He was a knight. A man of honor, without doubt. Only honorable men were chosen as knights. Dragons, it was said, were excellent judges of character.

He was also by far the most handsome man she had ever been near. And his attractiveness wasn't just skin-deep. The obvious love he had for his dragon friend showed in his every action. He had been polite, kind, funny and welcoming. Sexy too, though not in a blatant way...until just now. Her eyes were drawn by the erection he did little to hide.

Admittedly, his tunic covered him, just barely. But judging by the impression in the fabric, he could not have easily hid his generous proportions even if he'd tried. Her mouth watered at the thought of touching him. There.

"What is this?" She was baffled by her own reactions. She met his gaze, knowing her flushed face and wide eyes showed her confusion and probably her arousal as well.

"Whatever you want it to be, milady." His voice had turned

seductive and low.

On one hand, she wanted him to grab her and take the decision out of her hands, but on the other, she knew he was not the kind of man to force a woman into intimacy—even if she was ultimately willing. No, Silla would have to be bold and make up her own mind. There was no easy way out for her here. She wanted him—a miracle in itself—and yet she was afraid.

"I am not accustomed to this kind of thing." She looked down at her hands, knowing the heat in her cheeks only increased.

Brodie moved, turning so that both of his feet touched the floor and he was left sitting on the side of the bed, next to her. One of his large hands lifted to stroke her cheek, and she found herself leaning into his caress.

"Don't you think I know that? You are a special woman, Silla. I recognized that from almost the first moment we met. I know this is fast, but such is the way with knights."

He shrugged, and she wasn't sure what he meant about knights being faster than others. Perhaps it was the danger of the lifestyle they led? Maybe they seized every moment because they were in such constant danger? The thought made her cringe inwardly. The idea that he put himself in harm's way on a regular basis both frightened her and made her feel pride in him, in his calling.

He leaned closer, but made no move to claim her lips. She could feel the warmth of his breath against her skin, feel the heat of him along her side. She knew what he was doing. He was dangling temptation in her path and seeing if she would take that final step, bridge the small distance between them and take what she wanted. In that way, he would know it truly was what she wanted, not something he had persuaded. Silla was both glad of his care for her feelings and disturbed that she would have to make the move.

Dare she?

Oh, yes, she thought as she joined her lips to his. She most definitely needed to dare this one time. She might come to regret her choice tomorrow, but for tonight, she would live a dream. She would suspend worry and doubt, and share her body with a man too good to be true. Too good to be hers for any longer than the space of a single, stolen night.

She pushed him back down onto the large bed and straddled his hard body. Now that she had made her decision, she had become the aggressor—a role she had never played before but found she enjoyed immensely. She was careful of his wound. It would not do to make him bleed again. Not now, when pleasure was on offer.

She kissed him deeply, plundering and allowing her mouth to be plundered in return. All the while, her fingers were busy with the ties of his tunic, loosening the maddening knots that kept her from her goal—his skin. The more she could touch him, the better.

After a battle with the stubborn fabric, she finally was able to push the tunic up and over his cooperative shoulders. He lifted, helping shift the cloth. Her focus had narrowed to this one man, this huge bed and her desire to join with him in every way she knew how. At least for this one blessed night, never to be repeated.

His chest was heavily muscled and scarred like his legs had been. His arms had taken the worst of the cuts over the years, but though many, few looked as if they had been severe when made. The extent of his injuries distracted her for only a moment, but it was long enough for him to turn the tables.

Brodie rolled, switching places so that she was under him. He'd hiked up the skirt of her simple dress in the process so that it rode around mid-thigh on her. He took quick advantage, planting his knees between hers, using one hand to push the fabric of her dress higher. She wore little beneath, but he was left only in his trews, so she supposed they should be even. Once he rid her of her dress, she would be left with only the thin covering of her pantaloons.

How she wished all the fabric that remained was gone already. She wanted nothing to come between them. Not now. She was too primed. Too ready. She wanted him, inside her, pumping into her waiting, receptive body.

She helped him remove her dress, gasping for air as his hands cupped her bare breasts. She thought she could not want him more. She'd been wrong. As he played with her sensitive nipples, then bent to lick them and suck them into his mouth one at a time, she learned the real meaning of yearning.

A shock of ecstasy made her gasp as pleasure rolled over her in a wave that took her by surprise. He sucked hard on one breast while pinching the other gently in a repetitive motion that made her moan. No man had elicited such responses from her. Not ever.

He pulled back and smiled, and she knew he understood what was going on in her body. His eyes held knowledge that she did not understand and secrets that made him happy for some reason. She didn't question it, she only wanted more of the pleasure he had taught her greedy body. She had become a wanton, it seemed, and all it had taken was this man to bring it about.

"There are still too many clothes," he complained with a smile, nipping at the soft skin of her belly as he stalked lower over her body. His hands untied the little bows of her pantaloons and pulled them down, his mouth following their path with small kisses.

She was shocked when his mouth stopped at the apex of her thighs and the fabric continued its downward slide until it was gone from her body. He spread her legs and then his tongue did the most amazing things to her clit. She'd been taught about anatomy, of course. Every good healer knew the

183

parts of the body and their functions. But never had she fully understood the purpose of the clitoris until now.

Brodie taught her things about her own body that made her want to laugh, cry and scream in pleasure all at the same time. She came again—harder this time, though she would not have believed such a thing was possible—with his mouth on her pussy. Her body hummed and unbelievably, was ready for more when he sat up between her thighs and removed his trews.

And there he was. Magnificent. Large, erect, well-shaped and all for her. At least for tonight. That lovely cock would be the instrument of her pleasure, if the Lady blessed her with yet another new experience.

Silla had been bedded before, but never, it seemed, by such a skilled and caring lover. So far, this experience had been everything she had dreamed of. Everything she had never thought she would ever experience. Fairy tale stuff about which young women dreamed.

She reached for him, wanting to give him a taste of what he'd already given her, but he stopped her and moved out of range. Her gaze met his and found him smiling gently.

"This time is for you, my dear Silla. It is my time to prove to you what you are capable of. My time to try to convince you this should not be our only time. Maybe tomorrow I'll let you play." He shrugged, though the look in his eyes told her he was looking forward to letting her have her way with him.

"You want more than just this night?" she asked, dumbfounded by his words. Could he really want more than just this? She had not dared hope...

"I want you. Repeatedly. As much as you'll allow and more."

Could he be serious? He looked serious. She began to believe and a small flicker of hope took shape in her heart, a tiny ember that could either be nurtured into flame or left to die on the hearth. Only time would see which way it would go.

"I want you, Brodie. Will you come into me now?" She spoke in a soft voice, slightly embarrassed by the words, but wanting him to know how she felt.

The broadening of his smile was her answer as he moved back between her thighs, positioning himself between her slick folds. His tongue had prepared the way, it seemed, eliciting the response from her body that would allow easy passage for his large size.

She knew the theory of how their parts would fit and had experienced it several times, but never with such a big man and never when she was truly prepared. Never had she responded to any man the way she responded to Brodie.

He slid inside with only minimal difficulty and then just stayed there, filling her. His gaze sought hers and silent communication seemed to pass between them. His eyes asked if she was all right and seemed to find their answer in her expression.

She was more than fine, if truth be told. She was experiencing true desire for the first time in her life and enjoying the feel of him inside her, testing her limits, rubbing against hidden points that made her want to squirm.

It was delightful. And it only got more so when he began to move. A slow rhythm at first that built and built as he watched her every response. A catch in her breath earned her a growl of approval and an increase in the pleasurable assault on her every sense.

His manly scent enticed her. The sound of his grunts and growls made her passion rise higher. The sight of him rising over her, his body straining against hers, was a new dream come true. The feel of him inside her and against her gave her delicious goose bumps and his skin had an almost addictive, salty tang against her mouth.

She felt something monumental gathering inside her. Tension of the most delicious kind and much greater than anything she'd experienced before. Her pleasure increased along with his pace until he was ramming into her in short digs that made her keen on every stroke. She came with a cry wrenched from her soul as he tensed above her, his hot seed flooding her womb with his warmth.

She spoke his name like a prayer as she held on for dear life, her body spinning into the vortex of bliss she had never known. So this then, was what drove so many people. She thought she finally understood. And it had taken this special man to teach her. Brodie was dear to her. So dear.

She would have said she loved him, if she still believed in such things. But love meant pain in her experience and it never lasted. Still, she was immensely fond of Brodie and would willingly be his bed partner any time he crooked his little finger. She was already addicted to his touch. Addicted to the amazing pleasure only he had ever taken time to show her. Perhaps, she thought, only he could bring it.

A sobering thought.

Brodie withdrew after a long moment and reached over the side of the bed to her stack of clean cloths. Holding her gaze, he wiped between her thighs, cleaning her. It was an intimate act nobody had ever performed for her, and it had the odd effect of making her want him all over again.

Her body was buzzing anew with arousal when he slid his fingers inside her, rubbing up against a spot that made her moan. He captured the sound with his lips as he kissed her senseless.

And that was when she heard another man chuckle.

Chapter Five

"We fly here in the dead of night because we heard you were injured, and what do I find but your hand up a willing woman's pussy."

"Stars damn your hide, Geoff, you always had lousy timing," Brodie groused, breaking away from Silla's sweet kiss.

He kept her legs splayed and his fingers up her cunt for all to see on purpose, even though she tried to squirm away from him. If she was going to be their wife, she would have to get used to Geoff watching them fuck—and Brodie watching them fuck, for that matter. Better to see if she was up for it now, to avoid misunderstandings.

"This is Silla," Brodie continued. "She is special to me, Geoff, so be polite and I might even see if she's willing to bed you."

"What?" Silla's eyes widened, and Brodie knew he had some fast talking to do.

"Remember when I said marriage in the Lair involved two knights and one woman?" He waited for her to nod, even as he rubbed her clit with slow, deliberate action. "I want you to be my wife, Silla. Mine and Geoff's. Forever. For always. To have and to hold and fuck together and apart." He felt a rush of fluid coat his hands, and he knew the idea appealed. "Think about it, Silla. Two cocks to give you pleasure, two men to cherish you for all your days, two warriors and their dragon partners to protect you always, and two hearts to share your love."

"Are you serious?" Silla's words were breathed in a whisper so low he hardly heard it. But the renewed thrum of her body under his gave him hope.

"As serious as I have ever been in my life. Knights often know right away when they meet the woman who is meant to share their lives. It is a blessing of our kind. I knew earlier this evening that I had met my match. Geoff's too, though you don't know him yet. I would bet everything I hold dear that once you get to know him a little, he will feel about you the way I already do."

"What way is that?" Her breath caught as he increased the pressure of his fingers inside her channel. He lowered his head to kiss her nipple, drawing it to a peak that made her gasp before he answered.

"I believe I will love you, Silla." He phrased his declaration carefully, guessing from the description of her past that she was cynical about love, and had no belief in love at first sight. "Now please let me fuck you again before I explode, then we can sit down with Geoff and you can get to know him a little." He didn't wait for her reply, turning to Geoff and jerking his head toward the chair near the bed. "Sit down and be quiet. This won't take but a moment."

"You want him to watch?" she asked in a shocked whisper as Brodie settled between her legs once more.

He wasn't about to chance her leaving if he let her up even for a second. She needed to come again and again until she was used to his touch and addicted to the pleasure he could give her. This was also a test of sorts. Dragons were notorious exhibitionists. When the dragons took to the sky in their mating flights, they didn't always check to see that their human counterparts were in a private place first. Lair life was lusty, and unmated knights often ended up being voyeurs to some extent. It was accepted as a matter of necessity when living with dragons.

Would Silla be open to the experience? And would she be able to share herself with Geoff as she had done with Brodie?

This was the first step to finding out.

Brodie removed his fingers and slid his cock into her without much fuss. He was sure to spread her legs wide so Geoff could see as much as possible. He played with Silla's generous breasts as he pumped within her, mindful of the audience, which excited the inner exhibitionist all knights seemed to carry.

He noted the direction of her gaze. Several times she looked over at Geoff, blushing to the roots of her hair but excited all the same. For it was at those times when she met Geoff's very interested gaze that her body gave forth its nectar around his cock, lubricating his way. Oh yes, she was interested. She was responding very well to this little unplanned test.

Brodie slowed his pace, wanting to push her closer to her limits. He pulled her thighs over his and leaned back, cupping her breasts in his hands.

"Our Silla has lovely round tits, doesn't she, Geoff?"

"What in the hells are you doing?" Geoff asked in the privacy of their minds. It was a gift of their partnering with dragons that they could communicate silently with each other as well. *"You're going to scare her off. If she really is the one for us, we have to be careful how we handle her."*

"Oh, she is our mate, Geoff. I have little doubt of that. She can hear Phelan."

"Truly?" Geoff's tone held hope. *"She can bespeak dragons?"*

"Truly, brother. She can. She is our mate. It is time we taught her what that means."

Geoff stood and came over to the bedside. They were in the middle of the huge mattress, so there was room for the other knight to sit.

Geoff reached out and plucked at the nipple standing upright on the closest breast. Brodie still cupped her, but Geoff

189

tugged at her nipple, working together as they would for the rest of their lives—if Silla agreed.

"Very fine indeed," Geoff agreed. "But does she follow orders?"

"And you said I was pushing things? You really want to try your discipline games on her now?" Brodie complained to his fighting partner, who he knew occasionally liked a bit of kink from his bed sport.

"Why not? If she is the one for us, she will be excited by the idea, don't you think?"

"If this goes badly, I will never forgive you."

Geoff seemed to rethink his plan and bent to retrieve some of Silla's bandages. She'd left her satchel open wide so she could easily access things and Geoff was taking full advantage.

"Does milady allow you to command her pleasure?" Geoff asked aloud. "Does she trust you enough to let me tie her to the bedpost?"

Silla's body jumped under him and Brodie tried to read her expression. He bent, placing his lips next to her ear.

"Geoff is friskier than I, I'm afraid. He likes to play games, but he will not harm you in any way, my love. Nor will I. I promise you on my life. My word as a knight. Do you trust me? I will guide you and protect you, but you must trust me or we will not go any further."

"What are you planning to do to me?" The question came out frightened, but Brodie could hear the small quiver of arousal in her tone as well. And the way her sweet cunny clenched repeatedly around his cock told him she was excited rather than truly scared.

He kissed her cheek, nibbling on her earlobe. "I plan to love you and bring you the greatest pleasure you've ever known. Again and again. But only if you trust me. I will not let you come to harm. What say you?" He had to have her answer before he let this go any further. She was too important to him—to all of them.

"I consent, but if I ask you to stop, you must promise me that you will."

"I vow it." He kissed her again, loving the way she clenched around him. "Now, raise your arms. We are going to tie you up."

Geoff took the arm closest to him and quickly looped a bit of the soft bandage around her wrist, tying the other end to the headboard. Brodie did the same on the other side. He had to leave the warm heat of her pussy to do it, but they had time now. She wasn't going to bolt. At least not until she called a halt and they untied her. He had time to entice her, to explore her, to ravish her slowly.

Time to introduce Geoff into the play, in small increments. As much as she could handle, or would allow. The sooner the three of them got used to each other, the sooner they could cement the bonds to join their little family and the dragons could mate. Silla would be the link that held them all together. If they did this right. And if she agreed to be their wife.

A lot was riding on the next few hours.

Chapter Six

Silla didn't know why she wasn't running for the hills. A strange man was tying her naked to a giant bed, and she was letting him! What had changed about her sanity in the past hour that she would allow such a thing?

But the little devil of lust that had finally been awakened in her body was driving her to comply with anything Brodie and his fighting partner asked. She'd heard about the threesomes in the Lairs around the country and always wondered how that might work. Here was her golden opportunity to find out. And most shocking of all, Brodie even said he wanted her to be their wife.

She still couldn't quite believe that part. She had been a wife and never thought she would ever contemplate such a thing again, but she had never dreamed a knight—make that *two* knights—would want her for their mate. She didn't know what to think about that. But she definitely wanted to know more of the pleasure that Brodie had introduced her to.

She couldn't deny that Geoff's gaze fired her senses. Perhaps she had hidden exhibitionist tendencies after all. She never would have believed it, but when Geoff had stared at her pussy while Brodie had been inside her, the intent expression on his face had made her breathless. And when they'd both touched her breast at the same time, she'd felt greedy for more.

Brodie alone had been incredible, but the forbidden allure of having two men touch her at the same time was fast becoming irresistible. Could she actually be contemplating allowing the newcomer to not only touch her, but to take her as well? Something she wouldn't even have considered only an hour ago was easily becoming the most tantalizing thought imaginable.

How would it work? What would it feel like? Would she survive such a thing and would they still want her after they'd gotten a taste of her?

All questions she would soon know the answer to, if she let this continue.

When her hands were secure, they shocked her by moving to her feet. One on each side. Spreading her legs and tying her ankles to the rail at the bottom of the wide bed. There was quite a bit of give in the long bandages they'd used to tie her, so she could move a little. She could bend her elbows and, more importantly, her knees. She imagined all sorts of scenarios that required bent knees and just the carnal thoughts in her mind made her temperature rise higher.

When she was spread-eagled before them, Brodie sat naked on one side of her, Geoff fully clothed on the other.

Geoff held her gaze as he began to remove his leather jerkin. Lace by lace, she watched him untie the leather that protected him while in flight with his dragon partner.

Geoff had blond hair and bright blue eyes. He was a perfect foil to Brodie's brown-haired, brown-eyed handsomeness. Geoff was more rugged-looking, while Brodie was prettier, but both were built on the massive side, with bulging muscles and the scars of the warrior life. Geoff shrugged out of his leather jerkin and yanked the cloth tunic he wore under it over his head.

She was a little breathless as she got her first look at his well-formed chest and arms. He had fewer scars than Brodie, but that was probably because, as Brodie had told her, he was younger. Of course, they both looked about the same age— slightly younger than her, even though they were older in years and mileage, if their scars were anything to go by.

Geoff held her gaze as his fingers trailed down the skin of her abdomen and back up again to tease lightly around her breast, drawing circles. He then transferred his attention to what his hand was doing, observing her body as if he were looking at a sculpture or a piece of fine art. He played with her nipple until it stood upright, as if begging for his touch.

"When you are tied up for our pleasure, you will address us as Sir. Is that clear?"

His words took her by surprise, and she hesitated. Geoff pinched her nipple, making her squeak, though it didn't hurt so much as shock her.

"I said, is that clear?" he repeated, waiting for an answer, his fingers rolling her nipple, soothing and exciting all at once.

"Yes," she gasped.

He pinched her again. Harder this time.

"Yes, what?"

It took her a moment to focus as he returned to rolling her pointed nipple between his thumb and forefinger.

"Yes, Sir?"

He let go and moved his hand back. "Very good. Kiss it better, Brodie. She seems to like your mouth on her tits."

Brodie moved into her line of vision and smiled at her before sucking her breast into his warm mouth. He used his tongue on her, eliciting a moan of pleasure from her throat.

"Ah, yes, she does like you, Brodie." Geoff's voice claimed her attention, as did the hand that started a path from her navel down to the apex of her spread thighs. Geoff's light touch circled around her clit, sliding through the fluid that came forth at his touch, and she saw the smile on his face, though he didn't meet her gaze. He was staring intently downward and she realized he was studying her crotch.

Her face flamed. Nobody had ever given her such an intent

inspection in that area. It wasn't seemly. Yet, it aroused her a great deal. More than she would have ever credited.

Geoff moved downward while Brodie still applied himself to her breasts, and she felt Geoff's hands gently bending her knees and separating her thighs as far as they would go. He had full access now and he wasn't long in using it. Both of his hands went to her pussy, spreading the lips apart while his face drew close enough that she could feel the waft of his warm breath over her most sensitive skin.

He kept her spread while one finger teased her clit and then, without warning, he let go and one long finger plunged into her channel, sliding right up into her core. Hard, fast and unexpected. Combined with the way Brodie was licking and sucking on her breasts, she felt sensation wash over her in a wave of completion. A small completion, now that she knew what Brodie could bring her if he really tried, but completion nonetheless.

Geoff withdrew his finger and patted her curls.

"Good girl," he said softly, his face coming back into view.

He still wore his leather pants, and the sight of him kneeling near her head brought her back to full arousal. To have two such handsome men focused solely on her body—on her pleasure—was a truly amazing thing.

"Have you sucked Brodie's cock yet?" he asked unexpectedly.

"No...Sir." She remembered his rules just in time.

"No? I thought for certain he would have stuck it down your throat already." The crude expression added something naughty, in a good way, to the proceedings, oddly enough.

Brodie moved away from her breasts and sat at her side, reaching up to hold the fingers of one hand, as if reassuring her.

"We haven't had a lot of time together, Geoff." Brodie's voice sounded like a warning, and she knew he was looking out for her comfort.

"No matter. It is easily rectified." Geoff lowered his face so his lips rested next to Silla's ear and he spoke in a low voice, his breath puffing against the shell of her ear with every word. "I know you do not know me yet, but if we are meant to be a family, we will learn each other in time. The question is, will you let me fuck you tonight? I allow you to decide, Lady Silla. Will you suck Brodie's cock while I learn the heat of your core? Or will you suck me while Brodie reclaims what he has known once already? Or will I stand aside and allow Brodie to bring you to completion? Simply tell me what you desire and this you shall have."

Goddess, what temptation! Silla didn't know where these desires were coming from and didn't care to question. The touch of these two men had driven her to a place of desperation, a place of yearning, a place of need. She wanted it all. And even if it was just for tonight, she wanted them both. Let the morning take care of itself. Tonight she wanted the dream. The fantasy. The ecstasy.

Geoff waited, his face very close to hers. He lifted slightly, his gaze meeting and holding hers.

"What is it to be, milady?"

For the first time, she saw the vulnerability in his eyes. She understood a little bit more about this strange knight and knew she could deny him nothing in this moment. Tomorrow might be another story, but for now, she was his. His and Brodie's.

"The first thing, Sir," she found the nerve to answer in the barest whisper. She saw the fire leap in his eyes as her words found their mark.

Geoff lowered his lips to hers in their first kiss. A gentle kiss of reverence. A tender salute that turned molten as his tongue met and dueled with hers. She didn't know how long it lasted, but when he lifted his head, the room was spinning. She was dizzy with desire and drunk on him.

"You will never regret this, my dear. I vow it."

Geoff moved up to kneel at her side, his fingers working on the fly of his leather pants. He pulled them down, freeing an impressive erection, holding her gaze all the while. She wanted to lick him, to learn his taste, but he moved away, down to where her thighs were still spread wide apart.

She was surprised when his hands sought the ties that held her ankles, freeing her. Brodie freed her wrists as well and together they coaxed her to turn over onto her hands and knees.

The new position brought her head in alignment with Brodie's straining cock and suddenly, she wanted to learn its texture and taste against her tongue. She didn't give him warning, simply licking her way up his cock while he was distracted watching Geoff prepare her.

Geoff's hands spread her thighs and his fingers speared into her, drawing out her moisture while she sucked Brodie's cock deep into her mouth. He tasted salty and divine, while Geoff kept her off balance with the thrust of his fingers. They left and were soon replaced by his cock.

He slid in slowly, the curve of his long hardness making the feel of him somewhat different from Brodie. He pushed in and she realized his rhythm against her backside drove her deeper onto Brodie in front.

She liked it. The rhythm he set up pleased them all and before long they were grunting, groaning and straining against each other in an ever-increasing pace. When Geoff slapped her ass, she squeaked in surprise. It felt oddly good as she clenched on him, and he did it again, eliciting the same response. She couldn't take much of such treatment. It was too exciting. Too different and foreign to anything she'd experienced before.

She came in a rush and would have screamed if not for the cock in her mouth. Brodie came a moment later, pulling out of her mouth to shoot his come over her hanging breasts. She rose up slightly and pressed her breasts against him, prolonging the moment for them both. Geoff was still pumping within her when Brodie drew away, collapsing against the headboard, watching them.

Geoff's arms snaked around her and cupped her breasts, sliding in the come left there by Brodie, rubbing repeatedly over her nipples in a way that made her want to scream. Her climax extended, becoming two and then three orgasms while he continued to pound into her from behind.

When he tensed and squeezed her nipples hardest of all, she exploded one last time and felt the warmth of his come inside her, sliding, slipping and dripping as he continued to pulse in and out of her core. She did scream then, an incoherent sound of the most amazing pleasure she'd ever known. Made all the more alluring by the heated brown gaze of Brodie, watching them.

Dammit. Maybe she really was an exhibitionist after all.

Chapter Seven

They fucked all night long, singly and in triad, and finally found sleep a few hours before dawn. Silla woke as the first beams of light came in through the window, knowing she had to see to her patient. She slid out of the bed as quietly as possible. The knights had taken up positions on either side of her and did not stir as she dressed and slipped out into the early morning light.

She found two dragons where there had been only one the night before. They lay very close, their necks entwined. She paused to watch them for a moment. They looked so happy...

She saw now, in the morning light, that Phelan was a metallic bronze in color, while the female who lay close to him was so deep a blue, she was almost purple. Their colors were complementary and the shine of their scales was something she had not expected. Instead of leathery, they looked almost like polished metal. Yet they were supple and able to bend in ways she had not expected of creatures so large.

"Good morrow, Lady Silla," came the rumbly voice she'd heard last night inside her mind. Phelan was speaking to her, and she finally noticed his eyes blinking open.

"Good morrow, Sir Phelan. How do you feel today?" she asked aloud, not sure how to—or even if she could—reply the same way.

"I am well and happy. My mate is here and our knights report that we may soon be together again." The other dragon stirred and opened her eyes. They unwound their long necks and both giant heads rose a few feet in the air to stare down at

her.

As they moved, she noted the almost iridescent sheen of their scales as the light played off them. The dragon, who had been impressive in the lantern lit night, was almost overwhelming in the light of day. She wondered how magnificent he would appear when the sun's rays grew stronger and kissed his living armor.

"May I approach? Sir Brodie and I prepared more burnjelly last night that will make you more comfortable this morning, I believe." She held the bowls in her hands aloft for the dragon to see.

"Thank you for your care of my mate," came another voice in her mind. This one was somehow softer, though no less immense. It was the female dragon, speaking directly to her for the first time. *"I am Qwila."*

"I am Silla," she replied, cracking an involuntary smile when she realized their names rhymed. She saw the dragons chuckle as tendrils of cinnamon-scented smoke rose into the early morning air.

"It was my honor," she went on. "I am a journeyman healer of the High Temple of Our Lady of Light. Though I have never treated a dragon before, I am sworn to provide care to all of Her creatures, human and otherwise."

"We know of your Order," Phelan answered. *"Osric is a part of our extended family through Brodie. Osric would have made an excellent knight, if not for his penchant to heal things rather than demolish them."*

Again came the little spirals of smoke that indicated dragonish amusement. Silla found herself smiling as well. Phelan had summed up Osric's nature perfectly. A gentler man she had never met. It would be impossible for him to wield a sword, even in defense of innocents. He was a pacifist through and through.

"Your skills will be an excellent addition to our new Lair. We have no healer yet and would be hard pressed to find one of your skill willing to live and work with our kind," Qwila added. *"Believe it or not, many people are afraid of us."* Her tone indicated wry humor that Silla appreciated. Dragons really weren't scary at all, once you were able to speak to them a bit.

But Qwila was talking as if Silla's joining their little group was already set in stone. Silla still had doubts.

"May I?" she reminded the dragons, proffering the burnjelly bowls again.

"Yes, please," Phelan answered in her mind. He moved his wing slightly, so she could get as close as possible to the worst of his wounds. Qwila helped, using her own wing to prop his up and take some of the weight off the joint that had been damaged.

Phelan lowered his head to the ground, resting it on his forearms and closing his eyes. Qwila's head rose over Silla's, watching intently as she examined the wound.

"This has done better than I expected," Silla reported as she inspected the deep red gash that had begun to heal at record pace. "If it is not too painful for you, I will apply the burnjelly directly. It should make you feel much more comfortable as soon as it begins to absorb."

"Thank you, healer. I will let you know if I cannot bear the agony." Phelan's voice held a teasing note, and she realized she was treating him as she would her human patients. Undoubtedly the dragon's tolerances were quite different indeed.

"Forgive me, Sir Phelan. I see I have much to learn about your kind." She saw the amused smoke rising from his nostrils a few yards away and was amazed again at his sense of humor.

"Not to worry," Qwila's voice rumbled through her mind. *"You will have many decades to perfect your knowledge of how*

to treat our kind once you formally join your life to our knights, and by their connection, to us."

Silla's hands paused, then continued in their work. Phelan's wound required all the burnjelly they'd prepared and probably could have taken more, but she'd have to raid more of her plants in order to get it.

"I'm still not sure about all of this." She decided to be candid with the dragons, since they seemed to be under the impression she really was going to marry their knights. "I dare not believe it's real."

"It is as real as I am." Qwila's head lowered so she could look into Silla's eyes. The dragon seemed completely serious. *"You are the woman the Mother of All has chosen for our knights. For our family. You can hear us!"* She seemed particularly impressed by that fact. *"Do you know how rare that is?"*

"Um...no. Is it?" Silla felt unsure.

"Rarer than diamonds, my dear doubter," Phelan piped in, his head still reclining on his forelegs and his eyes still closed. *"We know you are the one. Our knights know it. It is only for you to understand and agree."*

"You make it sound so simple." Finished with her work on his wound, she stepped back so she could see both of the dragons at once while they continued their conversation.

"It is simple. Search your heart," Qwila advised. *"You know that deep down, you are already joined to them both. It is only for you to accept the connection and allow it to open wider so that it will never be closed. Through your bond to our knights, you will connect with us as well and our magic will sustain you for many, many years."*

"It seems incredible," Silla whispered, dropping her gaze. She felt at sea, lost to all the change that had come to her life in such a short time.

"It's real," Brodie's voice came to her from behind as he

moved in and tugged her back against him. His arms held her, making her feel safe in the sea of confusion that had surrounded her in the past hours since arriving in Bayberry Heath.

He kissed her temple, his arms around her waist. "I feel more in my heart for you, Silla, than I ever have for any other woman. Knights know their mate almost immediately. You are mine. And Geoff's. The fact that you can talk to these two only confirms it." Humor laced his tone as he referred to the dragons. "If you give us a chance, we will convince you that you truly belong with us for all time. As you know, we can be very persuasive." He turned her in his arms and the joy she found in his expression was enchanting.

Geoff walked up as Brodie let her go, and saying nothing, he took her into his arms, rocking her gently from side to side as he hugged her. Enfolding her in his tallness, his power, his strength. Far from being overwhelmed, she found she loved the sensation.

Almost as much as she loved him? Could she really love him—and Brodie—in so short an acquaintance?

Geoff's hug changed as he drew back and lowered his face to match his lips to hers in a sweet, gentle, unexpected kiss. When he drew back, she saw an unaccountable brightness in his eyes, as if he was almost overcome with emotion.

"I pushed you far last night. I did not believe love at first sight was real, even though many tales speak of such things between knights and their mates. Forgive me? I am convinced beyond the shadow of a doubt that you are the missing piece to our family. With you—and only you, dear Silla—can we all be happy. Will you do that for us? Will you make us the happiest of men, and allow our dragon partners to be together once more?"

"But what of my work?" She asked the first thing that popped into her mind. She didn't know what to say. The wild part of her heart wanted to jump into their arms and never look back, but her practical side was casting doubts. She had never been lucky in marriage before. She had resigned herself to living a life of service and solitude. Why should things change so drastically for her now?

Geoff smiled. "Your skills will be much in demand in the Lair. In fact, we will be lucky to see you at all once everyone knows you are a Temple-trained healer. Such things are rare in the outlying Lairs."

"And what about Hero? What's to become of him?"

"Hero? Who is that?" Geoff asked, clearly puzzled.

"My horse." But the old gelding was more than that. He was her friend, confidant, and had been her constant companion these past few years. She didn't want to leave him to the care of strangers.

"You named that old nag Hero?" Brodie chuckled from the side.

"He's not a nag. He's my friend, and I won't leave him behind."

"You won't have to, my love," Geoff assured her with a little squeeze. "He will have oats and hay and a warm place to live out his life. There is a stable built into the Lair for the beasts of burden we use to cart supplies. He will live there and you can see him every day."

"And my brother, Osric, will make things right with the Temple," Brodie put in, moving closer. Geoff stepped to her right to allow Brodie room on her left. They both took one of her hands. Geoff kept his arm around her shoulder, while Brodie looped one loosely around her waist. "The Temple's loss will be our gain. And if we haven't said it before, be assured Geoff and I will never harm you. We will never stray from you. You will be our touchstone and our guiding light. You are the woman we have been searching for. Only you, Silla, until the Mother calls us all home to Her Light."

Tears filled Silla's eyes as his words calmed her fears and made her hope. Did she dare trust these men? These knights of the realm?

Everyone knew there were no better men in the realm of Draconia than the noble knights who were chosen for their honor as much as their skill by magical dragons who could see into their very soul. Why did she doubt, when both Brodie and Geoff had already proven their worth simply by being chosen as knights?

They would not hurt her. They would not scorn her. They would never throw her out into the street. And everyone knew there was no such thing as divorce among knights and their mates.

Her fears laid to rest, Silla did the only thing she could do. She kissed each of her knights on the cheek and whispered the word that all four beings waited to hear.

"Yes."

About the Author

Bianca D'Arc has run a laboratory, climbed the corporate ladder in the shark-infested streets of Manhattan, studied and taught martial arts, and earned the right to put a whole bunch of letters after her name, but she's always enjoyed writing more than any of her other pursuits. She grew up and still lives on Long Island, where she keeps busy with an extensive garden, several aquariums full of very demanding fish, and writing her favorite genres of paranormal, fantasy and sci-fi romance.

Bianca loves to hear from readers and can be reached through Facebook, her Yahoo group or through the various links on her website.

Website:
http://biancadarc.com

Yahoo Group:
http://groups.yahoo.com/group/BiancaDArc/join

Hope returns to all dragonkind as
enemies become allies...and lovers.

Border Lair
© *2012 Bianca D'Arc*
Dragon Knights, Book 2

As a young widow, Adora raised her daughter by herself, never dreaming that love could cross her path again. But now that her girl is married to a pair of dragon knights, Adora's eyes are opened to all the possibilities the Border Lair has to offer...including two handsome men who catch her eye.

Lord Darian Vordekrais is about to turn traitor, giving up his title, his lands, and his home in order to warn the dragons and knights of his treacherous king's evil plan. But after he meets the beautiful widow, his sacrifice seems worth the cost. Meanwhile, Darian's old friend Sir Jared, who lost his first wife and child to treachery, is shaken by his own intense attraction to Adora. But Jared's broken heart is frozen in ice. Or is it?

As war looms on the horizon, the knights and dragons of the Border Lair rise to the occasion. New allies rally to their side, and romance blossoms and grows even as evil invades the land. The knights and dragons must stand fast against the onslaught, the beautiful woman of royal blood bringing them hope, healing and love.

Warning: This book contains a couple of meddling, matchmaking dragons who won't stop until two sexy knights realize the lady of their dreams can love them both separately and together. Ménage a trois and a bit of exhibitionism compete with the dragons for smoking hotness.

Available now in ebook and print from Samhain Publishing.

SAMHAIN
PUBLISHING

It's all about the story...

Romance

HORROR

www.samhainpublishing.com

CPSIA information can be obtained at www.ICGtesting.com
Printed in the USA
BVOW07s1442290813

329869BV00004B/172/P